THE GLASS PAINTING

An old forgotten masterpiece, a painting on glass, found beneath the ruins of an ancient French mansion, had belonged to the Marquis de Garac. When Emily Hastings' sister Irene inherits the painting, they are informed that it should be given a place of honour. Soon afterwards Irene becomes mysteriously ill and signs of imminent danger point towards Emily. A strange black cat haunts the house, and then the image on the glass painting begins to change . . .

Books by V. J. Banis
in the Linford Mystery Library:

THE WOLVES OF CRAYWOOD

V. J. BANIS

THE GLASS PAINTING

Complete and Unabridged

LINFORD
Leicester

First published in Great Britain

First Linford Edition
published 2013

British Library CIP Data

Banis, Victor J.
    The glass painting. - -
    (Linford mystery library)
    1. Suspense fiction.
    2. Large type books.
    I. Title II. Series
    813.5'4–dc23

    ISBN 978–1–4448–1508–5

Published by
F. A. Thorpe (Publishing)
Anstey, Leicestershire

Set by Words & Graphics Ltd.
Anstey, Leicestershire
Printed and bound in Great Britain by
T. J. International Ltd., Padstow, Cornwall

This book is printed on acid-free paper

PART 1

IRENE

1

Let none admire
That riches grow in Hell.
—John Milton

The telegram came first, before the letter, telling just enough to tease. Elliot and Irene Lewis could not believe what it told them, and they thought someone was playing a joke.

'What about that man you went to school with?' Irene suggested. 'What was his name, the one who went into law?'

'Winters?' Elliot suggested.

'Yes, that's him, Winters. Why don't you ask his advice? Surely he couldn't charge too much just to read a letter and give you some advice.'

The little sarcasm had been almost unconscious, but when she saw the scowl on his face she was sorry at once. She certainly did not want to provoke yet another quarrel, and money was a sore subject with them. Elliot was unhappily aware that if he set aside his own prejudices and accepted his wife's money, their lives would be greatly changed. He could pursue his ambition to be a writer, without the necessity of holding down another job. They could afford a better home than this flat they now lived in. They could even afford attorney's fees.

His scowl lasted only a few seconds, however, disappearing when his eyes fell again on the letter in his wife's hand. If what it said were true, they could have those things anyway, without demeaning his role as the family breadwinner.

★ ★ ★

'It's perfectly legitimate,' Irene said a few days later to her sister, Emily, who was in from California.

'Actually,' Elliot said, stirring martinis in an old quart jar, 'Winters didn't go quite that far. What he said was that the law firm in Paris was legitimate and highly respected, and that the letter, so far as he could tell, was authentic. On the

4

surface, it looks very much like we have inherited a house in France.'

Emily watched him refill her glass from the old jar and suppressed a smile. She had been along on an earlier visit when Irene purchased a perfectly good Waterford cocktail pitcher at Bergdorf's. It was so like Elliot to use this crude container instead.

'Thank you, darling,' Irene said as he filled her glass. 'What an ugly jar. Was that in our kitchen? Oh, is that a cat?'

'In your martini?' Emily asked, amused. She was used to the way her sister's conversation sometimes skittered from one thing to another. 'How many of those have you had, anyway?'

'Only one. Look, at the window there.'

They looked, but there was nothing at the window but the New York skyline beyond. 'You must be imagining things,' Elliot said. 'What would a cat be doing out there? We're nineteen stories up.'

Irene got up and went to the window and looked out. 'I thought I saw one,' she said, coming back to join the others. 'It was looking in, right at me, as if it were watching me.' She saw Emily's look and laughed. 'I'm not drunk,' she said, 'but if I were, I'd have a right. Who would have thought Elliot would have a rich aunt?'

'Yes, me of all people,' he said a bit dryly.

Emily, anxious to ward off a quarrel, asked, 'Who is she, anyway? Have you mentioned her before?'

'I doubt it,' he said. 'To tell you the truth, I had forgotten Aunt Margaret. I haven't laid eyes on her in twenty years or more, since I was a kid. I remember my parents mentioning her once or twice, and I've racked my memory. She was the family eccentric.

'I don't suppose I'd have inherited anything at all if there had been anyone else, but she and I must be all that's left of the family. The letter says if I don't want to accept the inheritance, the property is to be sold and the money divided up among some certain charities. Probably that's really what she intended to do, but when it came time to draw up the will, she remembered that my parents had a son, and thought she ought to give

6

me a chance at it if I wanted it.'

Emily lifted an eyebrow. 'If you don't want to accept it?' she asked. 'That sounds to me like there's some sort of catch to the whole business.'

'In a way, there is,' Elliot said reluctantly. 'The house needs some work.'

'How much work?' Emily asked.

'We don't actually know,' Irene said. 'The will provides for money to complete the restoration, if Elliot accepts it. Aunt what's-her-name hadn't ever lived in this place, it seems. Apparently she purchased it with the idea of restoring it and making it into her home, and never got around to it. So, we've got the project now, if we want it. If not . . . ' She shrugged.

Emily put her glass down with a loud clunk. 'But, Irene, you can't go traipsing halfway around the globe to a house you've never even seen. There's no telling what shape it might be in. It might be a hovel.'

'Aunt Margaret doesn't seem to have been the sort to invest in hovels,' Elliot said. 'And this gives us the chance we've been waiting for. We can live there,

7

without rent or monthly payments, and we can stretch my savings to last for the better part of two years. By then my writing ought to be making some money for us.'

'Anyway,' Irene asked, 'What are we giving up? All this?' She made a sweeping gesture that included the room they were in, with all its inexpensive furnishings.

Emily saw Elliot's unhappy reaction and she said quickly, 'I suppose I'm just jealous. It sounds great fun, really, in a way, to go off on an adventure. I wish I were going with you.'

Irene clapped her hands together like a little girl. 'But why don't you?' she asked. 'It would be so much fun with you along. You're so good at handling things, and I would have someone to talk to.'

'I wish I could,' Emily said with a shake of her head, 'but I've got so many things going on just now, I haven't got time to turn around. Besides, it will do you both good, to have the trip together, without me tagging along. It can be like a second honeymoon for you.'

Emily Hastings had reasons for not

wanting to accompany the couple to France, but not the ones she had given. All of them came down to one central point: she was in love with Elliot.

Of course, she had always kept that fact to herself. She loved her sister, too, and although she knew the couple had their share of discord, primarily over financial matters, and although she knew that Elliot could be a bit of a stick in the mud, she was convinced that his strong will and practical sense were good for the flighty Irene.

Emily had never let Elliot know how she felt about him, either. She had met him first, in a bookstore. He offered his opinion on a book she was looking over. They talked for a time and she invited him by for a drink the next day. She was smitten with him at once. He was such a sober, intellectual type, it never occurred to her that he would give a moment's notice to someone as frivolous as Irene, and she'd had no qualms about having Irene there the following day when he came by.

It was love at first sight for both of

them, and Emily, seeing at once how the wind blew, stepped quietly aside.

She was accustomed to such occurrences and did not resent them. She too thought her sister beautiful and enchanting, thoughtless though she often was; and she knew herself to be less than enchanting. She was approaching thirty and she was plain. She had a too-large mouth and little bright eyes and her nose was thin and freckled.

'I'll tell you what,' she said, seeing that Irene was already growing reluctant. 'We'll go on a shopping spree and get you completely outfitted for the trip.' She saw Elliot's frown, and said in a no-nonsense way, 'My treat. And as soon as you are settled in, I'll come for a long visit. Maybe I'll meet one of those dashing Frenchmen. This could be the chance of my lifetime, you know.'

Irene laughed and her good humor came back to her, but a little later, she grew thoughtful, and when Elliot was out of the room, she said, 'I hope this house is livable. Elliot is giving up his job to go. He's planning on burning every bridge.'

Emily suppressed her own misgivings about the plan, and said, 'It's probably a castle. I'll come for a visit and turn green with envy.'

By the time she left that evening, the Lewises were convinced they would be living in a castle in a matter of days.

2

They watch from their graves!
—Robert Browning

The house was not a castle, of course, although at one time it must have been quite handsome.

'It's in ruins,' Irene said. She did not try to mask her annoyance. She felt uncomfortably detached from home, from family, from country. They were in a strange land, and although Elliot's French was flawless and her own very good, it always irritated her to hear people talking in foreign languages when English would have served perfectly well. They'd had a long drive from Paris to get here. She was tired and unhappy.

And the end of all this was an old gray house that had an air of desolation about it despite the day's bright warmth. It was winter and it had rained from the time they started the trip until now. Today had started sunny and warm, and she had begun to feel more optimistic, but the sight of this house had certainly lowered her spirits.

The house was down a long narrow lane. There were no neighbors nearby — she had made note of that — but when they started down the lane, walking, since it was impassable for a car, she caught a glimpse of someone ahead, a man in a black suit.

'Look, there's someone waiting for us,' she said.

Elliot had paused to examine the ruins of what had once been a gatepost, which had long since crumbled to ruin. Now there was little more than two piles of stone on either side of the drive.

'How can that be?' he asked, looking up. 'The local agent is expecting us to come to his office, and no one else knows we're coming.'

'Well, he's certainly waiting for us,' she said. 'Look, right there . . . oh, where has he gone?' There was no sign of the man in black now, although the view was partially obscured. The trees along the lane had grown wild and all but blocked it in places, and it was overgrown with nettles.

Elliot resumed their stroll. 'Probably one of the local people, curious as to who we were,' he said. 'For that matter, maybe he knows who we are. We're probably big news here.'

Irene's spirits, already low, sank even lower when they came in sight of the house. It had obviously been uninhabited for many years, and was unquestionably a ruin. It was made chiefly of gray stone and it looked more like a barn just now than a great house. Over the big front door was a turret, and at one side a round tower covered in lichen. The red tile roof sagged ominously in several places.

'It's a beautiful thing, isn't it?' Elliot asked, looking like an excited boy.

'Elliot, you can't be serious,' Irene said, her dislike growing with every step they took. 'It'll fall down around us if we even try to step inside.'

'Nonsense. I'll admit it needs a lot of work, but that's all right. We've got plenty of time, and Aunt Margaret is footing the bill. But look at the lines. When it's restored it will be beautiful.'

Irene caught the note of determination in her husband's voice and bit her tongue. She knew he had made up his mind to accept the house, and her resistance would only make him more stubborn. He thought she was spoiled, and that she put too much importance on material things. It was true that she had a great appreciation for luxury. She did not like pinching pennies, or living in discomfort. She liked central heating and air-conditioning and plenty of ice for cocktails. She preferred a stereo system to a grand piano, and a big screen television to a country view.

It wasn't only the prospect of roughing it in this house that dampened her spirits, however. Despite her frivolous nature, she loved her husband with all the love of which she was capable. She would willingly, if not enthusiastically, follow him anywhere. She would prefer sleeping with him on silk sheets, but if it were a question of sleeping alone in luxury or on a floor with him, she would choose the latter.

There was something else here, though, that she could not quite put into words. It was the atmosphere that she did not like. It was like coming into a room that has been closed up for a long time. You cannot say the air smells bad, and yet you don't like breathing it.

The big front door of the house was locked. The key was with the local agent, who was waiting for them to show up at his office so he could show them the house, but they had come straight here, following the map they had been given at the law offices in Paris.

Elliot led the way enthusiastically about the house, holding aside weeds and nettles for his wife. The house was set on a bluff. There was a balcony with rusted iron railings, and some outbuildings. In the distance was what appeared to be an old watermill.

Irene shivered. It had been warm when they had gotten out of the car, but it seemed strangely cold here.

'I don't like this place,' she said flatly. 'I think we should turn right around and go back to New York.'

'And live where?' he asked impatiently. 'And on what?'

'You've got money in your savings account,' she said, knowing that it was a mistake to quarrel with him like this, but unable to keep her thoughts to herself.

'That wouldn't last us six months in New York City. And I haven't got a job now, don't forget, and they aren't all that easy to get these days. No, I think we shall stay right here.'

'Elliot, this place is obviously not habitable. Look at it. There must be a layer of filth a foot deep.'

'I'm sure there's a hotel in the village we can stay in for a few days, until we can get things in some sort of order. All we need is a room or two and we can live here while the restoration is going on. Come on, let's go look up that agent.'

Irene would have liked to dissuade him. She wanted to be back in Manhattan, with its skyline and its grimy buildings and its noisy streets.

She knew what it was like when Elliot made up his mind, however, and that it would be disastrous to argue with him just now, when he was in the throes of enthusiasm for this new project.

So she went quietly along with him, back to the car. She had an uncomfortable feeling of being watched, and twice she turned around quickly, expecting to see that man in black again, watching them, but there was nothing, only the old gray house, sitting poised and expectant, as if it had begun to rouse itself at the suggestion of occupants.

3

*Th' infernal doors,
and on their hinges grate
Harsh thunder.*
—John Milton

'There's that man again, watching us.'

Irene went to the terrace doors. She could see the figure in black in the distance, at the edge of the trees. It was too far to see his face, but it was clearly turned in this direction. And she was sure it was the same man, although she could not make out very much about him. There was something about the way he stood, perhaps — she couldn't say for sure, but she knew he was the same.

Elliot came to the doorway and said, 'Look, darling, this room will work out perfectly as an office for me. What's that? What man? I don't see anyone.'

'He was there, at the edge of the trees,' she said, pointing. There was certainly no one there now. In the seconds that she had turned to glance toward Elliot, the man had vanished.

'There's no one there now.'

'I know. He keeps disappearing, like he was hiding. Elliot, you don't suppose he *is* hiding somewhere on the grounds? What if he's an escaped criminal or something like that?'

Elliot chuckled and turned away from the doors. 'You know, sweetheart, sometimes I think with your imagination you should be the writer.'

'Well, it's no good laughing at me.' She followed him back inside. 'I have seen him, I tell you. That's the third time now. And there's something furtive about the way he keeps appearing and disappearing.'

'He's probably some local peasant who's been hunting birds on the estate, and is afraid we'll make him stop if we catch him.'

'And I certainly shall. I don't care to have all the local men walking around the grounds with rifles firing at every moving thing.'

'We'll have signs posted. Come here, look at this.'

Elliot's enthusiasm had not, as she had hoped, waned upon seeing the condition of the house's interior. Indeed, he had grown increasingly pleased. She still had some reservations, but his enthusiasm was contagious, and she could begin to see that the house did indeed have some possibilities.

They had made only a brief tour of the rooms when the agent brought them out. The man had been brusque, and seemed in something of a hurry to turn the house over to them and be on his way. That had suited Elliot fine. He preferred to look the place over at his own pace, and by now they were in possession of the house, free to do as they wished with it.

That it would make a splendid appearance when renovated could hardly be denied. One entered a small foyer and at once descended broad stone steps to enter a great stone hall, fully two stories high. The little windows high up left the chamber almost dark, but electrical wiring had been installed sometime in the past.

'Anyway,' Elliot pointed out, 'this was a room intended for shadows and the flickering light of torches. Look at that fireplace, you could roast a water buffalo in it.'

'I don't think they have water buffalo here,' she said. 'Do you suppose we can restore that gallery?' A wooden gallery ran across one end of the hall, but it was partially collapsed.

'Why not? It's Aunt Margaret's treat. Careful where you step.'

Elliot did not even try to count all the many rooms on this initial visit, but there were other reception rooms, and close to a dozen bedrooms upstairs. A splendid little studio off the great hall would work wonderfully for his office, and Irene was delighted by the vast kitchen.

To the rear, rusted railings enclosed a large tiled terrace from which the ground dropped away forty feet or so, to the edge of the woods. Above the trees one could see wooded hills and valleys and glimpses of a stream that emerged at an old watermill and mill house.

'You know,' Irene said, 'if someone

were hiding on the property, that mill house would be the logical place.'

Elliot laughed. He was in too good a mood to let her uneasiness dampen his spirits. 'Darling, I promise you, we'll go over the grounds very carefully, just so that I can convince you there is no one hiding on the property.'

'Laugh at me if you want but . . . oh, look, a cat.' A huge black cat had suddenly leapt up from below, appearing as if by magic upon the rusted iron railing. He sat in easy elegance, regarding them with gleaming yellow eyes.

'Huge beast, isn't he?' Elliot said. 'He must be as big as a good cocker spaniel.' He went to the railing and looked down at the patch of thick undergrowth below. 'I can't think how he ever got through all that to get up here.'

'Cats are great climbers.' She tentatively put out a hand. The cat bent his head a little, as if inviting her touch, and when she began to pet him, he set up a vibrant purring.

'He's beautiful,' she said. 'I wonder what he's doing here? Do you suppose he belongs to somebody?'

'He's probably hunting rats.'

'Ugh.' Irene made a face. 'In that case, let's encourage him to stay.'

The cat seemed to have the same idea. He jumped down from the railing and strode past them into the house.

'He seems to know his way around,' she said. 'Maybe he belonged to the previous owners.'

'I doubt that. The house has been unoccupied for forty years or more.'

'Look, there's a mist rising.'

It was dusk and they could hear the gentle tinkling of the water in the old mill and see a thin mist beginning to rise from the dark trees.

'Loads of atmosphere.' He slipped an arm about her.

'Loads of mildew.'

He laughed again. 'We're too far up. You've got to admit it gives the place a romantic atmosphere.'

Eerie was more the word, she was thinking, but she kept that thought to herself. Even as they watched, the white mist, like smoke drifting upward, moved up through the trees so that the furthest ones faded from sight in its clouds.

Irene still had reservations, but not as pronounced as they had been. She had to admit that the house did have possibilities; and if it made Elliot happy, then she must try to make the best of it. Already she was wondering what sort of television programming they had here in France, and whether any of it was in English, and would they need special equipment to pick it up down here.

It was rapidly growing darker. They went in, gathering their things together. They could just see well enough to find their way to the front door.

As they were going out, Irene said, 'Oh, that cat.'

'What about him?'

'We've left him inside somewhere.'

'He can get out the same way he came in. It's gotten so dark we'd have to feel our way around to look for him. Anyway, I got the impression he'd been here before.'

'Maybe he's come to stay.'

Elliot closed the door. He did not bother to lock it.

They had a bit of good luck in finding an architect to take on the restoration. They spent the night in a little hotel in the village, and the next day made inquiries. Almost at once they were directed to a Monsieur Bernard who lived in semi-retirement in the neighborhood and who was, it seemed, an architect of some international reputation.

They found M. Bernard in a surprisingly inelegant cottage at the edge of town. He was guarded by a ferocious looking woman who turned out to be his housekeeper, and four less ferocious dogs, one a Saint Bernard, and the others of mixed stock.

'The Bernard was a gift from a client,' he explained when they had been shown into the garden where he was seated. 'Two Bernards in one house, but only one of them is a Saint. You are the American couple who have inherited the Garac château?'

'Yes,' Elliot said, 'and to save time, we've come to see if we could interest you

26

in taking charge of the renovation.'

'An interesting house, that one,' he said. 'I have often noted it, and felt the desire to, how do you put it, to poke around inside. You shall have to tolerate my friends here.' He indicated the dogs with a wave of his hand. 'They are tyrants, with a great passion for architecture. If I try to leave them here, they shall wreak havoc on this place, and drive the housekeeper away, and since a good housekeeper is difficult to find, I must appease them by taking them along on my jobs.'

'Then by all means, let's have them along,' Elliot said. He was not a dog fancier, but he was so delighted at having a well-known architect in charge of the restoration that he felt positively enthusiastic about the dogs.

'I don't know how the cat is going to like that,' Irene said.

M. Bernard's face underwent a change. His smile vanished and his eyes narrowed. 'You have a cat?' he asked.

'Of course not.' Elliot looked puzzled. 'What made you say . . . ?'

'The big black one that came in yesterday,' Irene said.

'Lord, I'd forgotten that.' Elliot turned back to the Frenchman. 'We seem to have inherited one with the house. He came in from the woods yesterday, and made himself at home.'

'Ah, well, that is a different matter,' M. Bernard said. 'We do not like cats, my friends and I. Of course, if you meant to keep this one as a pet . . . ?' He cocked an inquiring eyebrow.

'It never entered our minds,' Elliot said quickly. 'I've been wondering how to get rid of the beast.'

M. Bernard's face brightened again. 'Ah, my friends shall soon resolve that question. Very well, *mes amis*, I shall take charge of your house. And now, I am eager to begin poking around.'

4

Some evil beast hath devoured him.
—Holy Bible,
Authorized King James Version

It was another bright sunny morning. In
the orchard below the terrace only a few
tendrils of mist remained, like ghostly fingers caressing the trees. The tinkling of
the water in the mill sounded more cheerful and less melancholy than it had yesterday.
The house was a shambles, it was true,
but it somehow seemed less objectionable
than it had before. There was still debris
everywhere, and the dirt, and the linger-
ing odor of decay assailed the nostrils. Yet
all in all, Irene found the house more
attractive than she had before.

'I suppose,' she told herself, 'it's
growing on me. In a month's time I shall
love it wildly.'

'These tiles are treasures,' M. Bernard
said, scraping away the lichen that had

grown over them. 'I would say they are Spanish, or Moorish. You run into that here in the South of France. The South of France has as much in common with the Spanish coast as it has with Paris — the climate, the food, the general lifestyle. Take that wrought iron on the balcony: Spanish, everyone would say, but not at all. It's quite typically French, from this region.'

The three of them began to carry out some of the debris, flinging it over the railing of the terrace. M. Bernard fetched buckets of water and in an hour's time they had cleaned most of the tiles.

'We'll have dinners by candlelight, right here on our own terrace,' Elliot said. 'It will be wonderful, with the mill over there and nothing but nature at our shoulders.'

'Lovely,' M. Bernard agreed. 'I shall come and prepare your first dinner myself. I do a superb dish of tripe, and there is a local wine here that you will find very pleasant.

Even Irene found herself looking forward to that first real dinner in their new home. For the first time she thought of it as their home, and not just a house.

This reverie was interrupted by a frightful ruckus from inside. The dogs, who had been exploring on their own, began to howl and bark.

'They've found the cat,' Irene cried as they went into the great hall.

The dogs had indeed found the cat. At that moment, the black creature was atop a huge pile of rubbish in one corner and the dogs were at its base, barking and yelping. They made feints at the heap but each time the cat bared teeth and claws and hissed so savagely that the dogs fell back.

'This looks like blood,' Irene said. 'You'd better call them off and let me put the cat out.'

Before this suggestion could be put into effect, however, the big Saint Bernard finally summoned the courage to scramble up the rubbish heap. He made a lunge for the cat, and gave a cry as a claw raked his nose. He retreated slightly, but now the challenge had been given, and the fight was on. Again he lunged, and the snarl that the dog gave was murderous.

'He'll kill the cat,' Irene cried.

The cat apparently had come to the same conclusion. Again his claws forced the dog to back off, and before another attack could be launched, he made a desperate lunge for one of the little narrow windows high up in the wall. It was an incredible jump, twelve feet or more. Somehow he made it. Glass broke, and the cat was gone.

The dogs howled and yapped with frustration, jumping up toward the window that they could not possibly reach.

'The poor cat must have killed itself in that fall,' Irene said. She gave her husband an anguished look, but M. Bernard looked less concerned.

'It is as well,' he said with a shrug. 'You could not have had my friends and the cat here together, that is obvious.'

'I'll go have a look outside,' Elliot said. 'You show M. Bernard the rest of the house.

Outside, however, he found no trace of the cat. The window the cat had jumped through faced on the side of a steep incline. There was plenty of broken glass below but there was no sign of the cat. Stooping, he looked at the fragments of glass and found blood on one of them. The cat had indeed hurt himself, it seemed, but not so badly that he had been unable to run away.

Elliot looked in the direction of the orchard. He thought he had a momentary glimpse of something black scurrying into the trees, but it was gone so quickly that he could not be certain he had seen anything at all.

'The cat seems to have gotten away,' he said when he came back in.

Irene looked relieved, but M. Bernard was philosophical. 'He will be more comfortable elsewhere, I think,' he said. 'Let us see what the upstairs chambers hold for us.'

Irene thought the Frenchman was being a bit callous, and that his dogs had behaved like brutes, but she bit her tongue. The damage was done, the cat was gone, and would undoubtedly not return, and M. Bernard had made it clear that if they wanted his services, they would have to tolerate the company of his dogs. She resigned herself to the fact that she would be spending a great deal of her upcoming time in the company of the four canines.

They spent that afternoon making plans with M. Bernard, deciding what work needed to be done right away, and what could be looked upon as long-range projects. There was discussion too of the costs, which necessitated a telephone conference with the law firm in Paris, and an appointment for a trip to Paris in a few days, to work out details regarding payment. The lawyers were to handle all of the payment themselves, although they seemed to place no restriction on the amount to be spent.

However, their luck in obtaining the services of M. Bernard was not without its drawbacks. The Frenchman was all for restoring the house in its original state. At the mention of plumbing, he balked.

'The de Garacs lived here for centuries without the benefit of plumbing and electrical appliances. No, we shall have it as it was.'

'The de Garacs probably had a

houseful of servants,' Irene pointed out. 'And they didn't know about such things as electrical appliances and bathrooms, but I do, and I am accustomed to having them.'

Elliot finally managed a compromise between the two of them. Since the electricity was already there, it might as well remain, and there would be one bathroom provided in what had been a large closet.

'Later, we can install all the bathrooms we want,' Elliot told his wife. 'Let's humor him for now, all right?'

It was agreed that in the morning they would come by for M. Bernard at his cottage, and the three of them would then hire the men to do the actual work. M. Bernard had drawings to do, and a great deal of planning, but in the meantime there was several days' work involved in just cleaning out debris and in preparing rooms so that Elliot and Irene could stay there rather than in the local hotel.

When they arrived in the morning at M. Bernard's cottage, however, it was at once apparent that something was amiss.

The housekeeper looked as if she had been crying, and when she opened the door and saw who it was, she ushered them silently in and indicated the sitting room.

They found M. Bernard there, his head in his hands, sobbing volubly.

'Ah, I cannot work today,' he cried when he saw them. 'Tragedy has struck.'

'What happened?' Irene cried. 'Has someone died?'

'Someone? You say someone?' He threw his hands dramatically into the air and turned his face up to Heaven. 'No, it is *someones* who have died. There, in the garden. See for yourself.'

He began to sob again. 'Let me go see,' Elliot said in a low voice, but Irene followed him to the doors that led to the little garden.

It was necessary to go no further. Even from the door they could see the carnage beyond. The four dogs lay about the garden, all of them dead, but it was not just that they were dead. They had been killed in some savage manner, their bodies ripped limb from limb. There was blood and torn flesh everywhere.

'Oh, Lord,' Irene gasped. Her stomach gave a warning turn and she clapped a hand over her mouth.

'My God,' Elliot said. 'But who . . . what could have done this?'

'I do not know,' M. Bernard sobbed behind them. 'It must have been a monster, a demon from hell. Look at them, all four of them healthy and ferocious. They could have taken on a saber-toothed tiger, and they have been ripped to shreds, as easily as if they were helpless little kittens. It is surely an act of the devil.'

'When did it happen?' Elliot asked.

'During the night. I can't think how I slept through it. You can see there must have been a terrible fight. You would think the noise would have roused the dead, but I heard nothing, and neither did that stupid fool of a woman who works for me. It is as if they lay down silently and let their throats be torn open.'

He began to cry and wail again, burying his face in his hands. It was plain no work could be done today and, after expressing their sympathy, Irene and

Elliot left, both of them quite unnerved. They went back to the café outside their hotel and had brandy with their coffees.

'I can't think why anyone would do such an awful thing,' Elliot said. 'It must have been a madman. Or someone with a grudge against M. Bernard.'

'Or against the dogs,' Irene said. She had meant only that people often did become disgruntled with the dogs of others, because of their barking or the mess they left behind, or because the dog has attacked them at some time. She had no sooner made the remark, however, than she remembered the scene the day before, with the dogs and the black cat.

'If it were possible for a single cat to do that damage, I'd suspect that big black cat. He had murder in his eye yesterday.'

'Except it couldn't have been a cat,' Elliot said. 'Or an animal at all, I'd be willing to bet. Because if an animal or animals — supposing there were something big enough and fierce enough to do that — had gotten in there and started fighting with the dogs, there would have been enough of a ruckus to arouse not only M. Bernard, but half the village as well. The best I can guess is that the dogs were somehow poisoned, or drugged. Maybe the housekeeper was bribed to help. Then, while they were asleep, someone came over the wall and did that to them.'

'How bestial, to attack and maim sleeping and helpless animals. I can't believe any man could do that.'

'Well, it had to be a man. Or men.'

'Unless M. Bernard was right.' He lifted an eyebrow quizzically. 'Unless it were a demon. An act of the devil.'

5

I could a tale unfold
whose lightest word
Would harrow up thy soul,
freeze thy young blood,
Make thy two eyes, like stars,
start from their spheres . . .
—William Shakespeare

Irene found herself thinking, it was almost as if their project was doomed from the beginning, as if it was not meant to get underway.

The tragic deaths of M. Bernard's dogs was only the beginning. It was impossible for him to work that day, of course, and though the Lewises were eager to begin, they were not unsympathetic people and they understood how he felt.

In any case, after the sight of the carnage in the architect's garden, neither Elliot nor Irene felt particularly like throwing themselves into cleaning away a

40

lot of filthy rubbish. They decided instead to spend the day strolling around the little village, which was, after all, to be 'their town.'

It was a charming town, of no great significance. It had no famous castle, nor so far as they could determine had it been the site of any famous battles or treaties. The church, while pleasant enough, did not look like any architectural marvel, and none of the restaurants they saw gave any indication of being renowned or Michelin recommended, though they heard of a two star restaurant in a nearby town.

In short, it was a pleasant town like hundreds of others, but when they had ended their day of touring it, they shared a vaguely distasteful feeling of having wasted time that could better have been spent in other ways.

On the following day they again went to see M. Bernard. He was barely civil to them, and they did not even bring up the subject of the work to be done, but only inquired after his health, exchanged a few polite remarks, and left.

On the day after that, when they again

went to the architect's cottage, he opened the door to them himself, and brought them into the parlor, where the housekeeper quickly served them coffee.

'Yes, yes, let us get on with the work,' he said brusquely when Elliot brought the subject up. 'Always I have hated unfinished projects. They weaken the character and undermine the talent.'

So it was agreed that they would start work that very day. Irene, though, retained some reservations. She could not help but see that, although the architect threw himself into the task of getting a work crew together and organizing the actual renovation of the house, the situation had changed from what it was initially.

M. Bernard had lost all the enthusiasm he had originally had for the project. He came to it now as if he were going into battle. He was aloof and even surly, with the workmen as well as with Irene and Elliot. She could not help feeling he somehow held them to blame for his tragic misfortune, and although she felt sorry for him, she thought his attitude grossly unreasonable.

As a result, she felt frankly uncomfortable with him. Elliot suggested that perhaps she would be happier leaving the work in his hands and the hands of M. Bernard, and she was happy to comply. She remained in town and contented herself with a daily visit to the house to see how the work was progressing.

The work was not progressing, however. It may have been that M. Bernard's attitude somehow changed the atmosphere of the place. The workmen had no sooner arrived at the house than they began to quarrel and bicker among themselves. Nothing would satisfy. It seemed as if all of their time was spent in heated argument, with themselves or with M. Bernard, or with Elliot, who quickly began to lose patience.

Half the men quit the first day, with no more rational explanation than that they 'did not like the air in the place.' The first day passed, and the second and virtually nothing had been accomplished. Irene bit her tongue. Once, she made some idle remark to Elliot and he nearly took her head off.

'If you think you can do it faster on your own,' he said sharply, 'I'll fire M. Bernard and the workmen, and you can take it over.'

After that she left the house to him, and spent most of her time in the village. This was how she came to make the acquaintance of the local abbé. She was having coffee at the café outside the hotel one day, and he came up to her table and introduced himself.

'May I join you?' he asked, indicating the chair opposite her. She nodded, a bit hesitantly, because she was always nervous in the presence of a man of the cloth.

There was nothing particularly ferocious about this plump little man, however. He had a warm and frequent smile, and when he laughed his whole body shook.

'You're the American woman who has taken over the de Garac château,' he said when he had ordered a coffee for himself.

'My husband inherited it, actually,' she explained. 'It belonged to his aunt. Perhaps you knew her?'

'No, no, not at all,' he said. 'I knew that the château had been purchased some years ago, and was to be renovated. Several starts were made, in fact, but nothing ever came of it. It seemed that every time it was decided to go ahead with the plan, something happened to delay matters, and eventually it looked as if she had quite given up the idea altogether. Then we heard that you and your husband were coming. Everyone has been curious to see if the château was finally going to be put in shape.'

They talked for a few minutes more and she found herself relaxing in the abbé's company. He was easygoing and pleasant and obviously very much enjoyed a chance to gossip. He told her an amusing anecdote about M. Bernard and the wife of the local baker, and another about the hotelkeeper at this very hotel.

'You've lived here all your life, then?' she asked.

'Yes, I was born not far from here. When I was a little boy I kept cows in a pasture just over that hill. Like Saint Joan, but I had no visions. I was much too wicked, and anyway my father would have whipped me if I had told of seeing or hearing things.'

'I doubt that he had to do that often.'

His eyes twinkled at his memories. 'Oh, but he did. I was a naughty boy, I confess that now. It shames me to think of some of the pranks I did then. My poor father must have given me up for hopeless.'

Irene laughed again at the image of this plump, aging priest as a wayward child. Yet there was something still childlike in him. He had about him the scent of the countryside in autumn when the crops are in, and the hay mown, and the trees are thick with apples. He lacked the tragic and austere saintliness known to so many men of the cloth, and had instead a simple infectious gaiety.

'You must know a great deal about the château, then,' she said.

His face darkened, and he glanced away from her. 'It has been empty for a long time now. Forty, fifty years, I should guess.'

She sensed he was evading the subject, and it made her press for a more direct answer. 'And before that?'

He shrugged and looked a little uncomfortable. 'Before that I was only a child, of course. There were stories . . . ' He paused.

'Heavens, you make it sound terrible. Is the place haunted, is that what you are afraid to tell me? Am I to watch for the headless figure of a man who appears at midnight?'

She meant this to be amusing, but the abbé did not look at all amused. He looked, in fact, altogether unhappy. 'The place was infamous. The de Garacs had an awful reputation. As I say, I was only a child, and of course my parents were not likely to sit down and tell me everything in detail, but a child hears things, and I would have had to be dense not to hear quite a bit. There were all sorts of stories, many of them no doubted exaggerated, of parties — you understand, licentious things.' He looked embarrassed.

'Father, I'm not ignorant of such matters.'

His face reddened a little, but he went on. 'There were stories that the last

47

Marquis de Garac was in league with Satan himself. It was whispered that he abducted local girls, and girls from the other villages nearby, and took them to his house to use in vile rites.'

'Surely that was exaggerated.' Far from being frightened by the infamous past of their new house, Irene was fascinated and amused. It would delight Elliot, and she was not one to put much truck in witchcraft and such. She had never really given any thought to what she believed in, except that she believed you could buy anything that anybody could possibly want at Bergdorf's or at Bloomingdale's.

'No doubt there was some exaggeration,' the abbé said. She saw that he took this entire business very seriously, and she cautioned herself not to be flippant. She would not want to hurt his feelings.

'And yet,' he paused again. 'There were a number of girls who disappeared mysteriously during that time. They have never been found. One cannot help but think . . . '

'They might have just run away from home. Girls do that. Or it could have been coincidence.'

'It might have been coincidence.'

She was determined to pump him for more of the story. It was too colorful to just let lie.

'When did this last Marquis die?'

'Quite some time ago — forty or fifty years ago, as I say. He did not die a saintly death, I am afraid.'

'How did it happen?'

'A young girl, the daughter of a local farmer, was walking home one night. She had been in the village late, and was coming along the road that leads past the fields of the château. Her father, a bad-tempered man, had decided to come looking for her. A man in black, wearing a hood that concealed his face, attacked the girl. He tried to drag her into the woods, but the father was close enough to hear her screams and came up in time to shoot the attacker. It turned out to be the Marquis.'

'Well, I must admit, he doesn't sound exactly genteel,' Irene said. She thought the abbé was growing too morose. Of course what had happened was ugly, but this was all over and done with so long ago, it hardly seemed worth getting serious about now.

'What happened to the house after that?' she asked. The abbé had lapsed into a thoughtful silence.

'It passed briefly into the hands of a distant cousin, who lived abroad, and who sold it to a Count from Paris. The Count came at once and took over the property. He stayed one night at the house and left the next morning, never to return.'

'Ghosts?' Irene asked, not altogether seriously.

The abbé looked uncomfortable again. 'No explanation was ever given. After that, the property was put up for sale and remained in neglect until your aunt purchased it. Then, after the false starts at renovation, it was abandoned again, until now. I have always wanted to see it at close range, and to go into it, but no one from around here ever dared to do so. In all this time I doubt that more than a half dozen local people have been inside the château.'

Signaling for the bill, Irene said, 'That's easily rectified. Why don't you come out with me now and have a look? I'm due for my daily visit.'

'I would be delighted. If you think your husband will not mind my presence.'

'No more than he will mind mine,' she said with a wink. 'Come along. You will save me from a scolding.'

6

Is there no baseness we would hide?
No inner vileness that we dread?
—Alfred, Lord Tennyson

The driveway had been cleared, and they parked in it, behind a battered old truck that belonged to the chief of the work crew, and set out on foot toward the house. They could see Elliot in front of the château, in conversation with another man. Irene thought that there was something about the other man that was familiar, but she could not immediately put her finger on it.

It came to her finally: the man was dressed in black, and when he changed his stance, she suddenly realized that he was the man she had seen watching them from a distance. It gave her a queer sensation to see him now, talking with Elliot.

The man in black turned, and saw her approaching with the abbé. He said something to Elliot, and both of them looked in her direction. Seeing the stranger watching her, she was more than ever convinced that he was the same man.

'I see you've found him,' she said as she walked up.

The two men looked puzzled. 'Have you been looking for me?' the stranger asked.

'Haven't I seen you before, at a distance?' Irene asked. This was the first time she had seen him up close, and he did not make an attractive appearance. His skin was as pale as death, the more so in contrast to the stark blackness of his suit, which was out of date. He had a wasted look. If the story of one's life can be said to be written upon the face, then his had been a busy and not an entirely nice life. There was something familiar and grating about even his slightest look or gesture.

'I do not think so,' he said. 'You are Mrs. Lewis, are you not?'

Elliot stepped into the breach. 'Darling, this is . . . ' He hesitated.

'Monsieur Philippe Gastion,' the stranger said, bowing low in an old-fashioned gesture. 'At your service.'

'My wife,' Elliot finished lamely.

Irene said, 'How do you do,' politely and introduced the abbé to her husband and M. Gastion. She turned to Elliot and said, 'I seem to be mistaken. I thought you had found our hiding man.'

'My wife thinks she has seen someone at a distance, watching us,' he explained. 'She thought we had a dark figure hiding from sight for some reason or other.'

'No doubt that is true,' M. Gastion replied.

Irene was at once interested. 'Do you think so?'

'I think for each of us there is another self, a dark self, hiding from sight,' M. Gastion said, somewhat portentously. 'Perhaps your hiding man is within you. Don't you agree, Monsieur Abbé?'

'There are different schools of thought on that,' the abbé said cautiously, 'but, yes, there are those who say that the devil exists within each of us, a darker self, sometimes taking command.'

Irene had lost interest when she realized that M. Gastion was speaking philosophically and not literally.

The conversation was interrupted by the appearance of M. Bernard. The architect looked angry. With no more than a brief nod in Irene's direction, he launched a verbal attack directed at Elliot.

'It is no use,' he said loudly. 'Those urns cannot remain. They shall ruin the entire effect. I absolutely refuse to allow them to remain where they are.'

'But they must have been there originally,' Elliot said. 'And if we're to restore the place as it was . . . '

'They could not have been there,' M. Bernard interrupted him, fairly shouting, 'the proportions are entirely wrong.'

'Can I help?' M. Gastion asked. His voice was quiet and silky in contrast to the other two. 'I know a little about these things.'

'It's a pair of metal urns we found in the great hall,' Elliot said. 'I felt that they must be part of the original furnishings and so they should remain, but M. Bernard disagrees.'

'One has only to look to see that they are all wrong,' the architect insisted.

M. Gastion smiled as if upon a pair of noisy children. 'Why do we not go and look at them.' He held out his hand to

Irene. 'Dear lady?'

At the sight of his hand, she gave a little gasp. 'You've been hurt.'

His hand was badly scarred. It looked as if the flesh had been raked by several pairs of strong, sharp teeth. The wounds had been washed, but not dressed.

He glanced down at his hand. 'It is nothing,' he said. 'A mean dog set upon me. Quite a vicious animal. It had to be killed.'

Irene's saw M. Bernard blanch at this remark, coming so close as it did to his own tragic experience. Of course M. Gastion could not know of that.

He had taken her arm. She had an ugly feeling of revulsion at his touch. Her skin felt as if something were crawling over it.

She pulled her shoulders back stiffly and, not wanting to be rude, said, 'Yes, let us go see these bones of contention.' With M. Gastion at her side, she led the little group inside.

The urns in question were actually a pair of iron pots, rustic but not without a certain charm. They were placed now on either side of the massive fireplace, and it was evident that M. Bernard was right.

'They look lost in this room,' Irene said a bit reluctantly. 'They're just too small, I'm afraid.'

'But they must have been done for this room,' Elliot argued. 'Look, their ironwork matches exactly with those brackets over there.'

It was true, the urns did seem to be matching pieces to a pair of huge wall brackets that flanked the great fireplace. From their design, the urns looked as if they belonged where they were, but the proportions were quite obviously wrong.

'You are both right, of course,' M. Gastion said. 'The urns were designed for this room, but they were not used where they are sitting now.'

'We've tried them against all the walls and in every corner,' Elliot said, a little sharply. He did not seem to like the other man's interference.

'But you haven't tried them where they used to be. Look for yourself. Their proportions are just right if you put them here.'

He strode to one of the urns and lifted it quite effortlessly, although it was evident the pot was very heavy. He carried it to where the rotted gallery ran across the one end. Turning toward them, he lifted the urn over his head, to the place where it would be if suspended from the gallery above.

'You see,' he said, his voice echoing the length of the great hall, 'they were used as braziers, to supplement the light and heat of the fire at that end. And their size is just right for this area under the galleries.'

'He's right,' Irene cried, clapping her hands together. 'But however did you guess that?'

M. Gastion put the pot down on the floor and came back toward them, brushing his hands upon his trousers. 'Quite simply, I used to come here when I was a child, and I remembered them clearly. They fascinated me because I was too little to be able to see the flames within. I could only see the flickering light they cast.'

The abbé, who had been silent all this time, said, 'You are from this area? Do I know you then?' He looked puzzled.

M. Gastion gave his head a shake. 'No, kind Father, I lived some distance away. My father was a friend of the de Garacs. As my mother was dead, I was sometimes brought along on visits.'

'From what I've heard, this was hardly the place for a child,' Irene said.

M. Gastion shrugged. 'I can't say. It was certainly fascinating, and if anything unusual or wicked went on, my eyes were carefully shielded from it. But my father lost his life in an accident and I went to Paris to live with a cousin there. I began at once to learn his book business, since my cousin had no children of his own, and I never seemed able to arrange a visit here again, until now. A vacation brought me south, and I could not resist coming here to see this scene from my childhood.'

His eyes went about the room in a nostalgic way. 'I am pleased that you mean to restore the house as it was. It was beautiful.' His face suddenly brightened. 'But perhaps I can help,' he said, turning back to Elliot. 'There must be other matters in doubt, questions of what the place was like. I may not be able to answer them all, but as you can see, my memory is good. I had planned on going to Marseilles, but there is nothing in particular to take me there. I would be far happier in one of the rooms here.'

'That is out of the question,' M. Bernard answered for the Lewises. 'The rooms are not yet livable.'

'But it would take so little to make one of them up. My needs are simple, really. If I had a place to sleep, I could take my meals in the village.'

'I'm afraid it would be awkward,' Elliot said, 'But thank you for your kind offer.'

M. Gastion seemed about to argue the point, but instead he gave another shrug. '*Bien*,' he said, 'but you will surely not object if I take a room locally and watch as the restoration goes along? I will promise not to get underfoot.'

His eyes met Irene's and again she had that feeling of revulsion. There was something disgustingly intimate in his glance. He seemed almost to be smirking, as if they shared some filthy secret between the two of them.

She looked away, coloring slightly. 'It's one and the same to us,' she said, 'if M. Bernard does not mind.'

'Just do not get in the way,' the architect said gruffly. He looked out of sorts, perhaps because he had been proven wrong over the question of the urns. Irene could not help noting once again that the work was not progressing. Virtually nothing seemed to have been done since her last visit. She would have liked to say something about it, but she knew this would provoke a quarrel. Instead, she said to the abbé, 'Perhaps you'd like to see the rest of the house?'

They excused themselves and went off on their tour of the house. M. Gastion seemed to have attached himself to Elliot and M. Bernard. When last she saw them, he was following the other two on their way to the terrace.

He was still with them when, an hour or so later, she and the abbé prepared to leave.

'Oh, by the way,' she said to Elliot, remembering, 'I forgot to mention that Emily is coming.'

'Emily?' Elliot said, looking pleased for the first time since she had arrived. 'Wonderful. When will she be here?'

'In a week or so. She decided to visit friends in Paris, and she thought she might as well make a swing down our way.'

'You seem delighted by the prospect,' M. Gastion said. 'This is an old friend?'

'My sister,' Irene said, 'And I am delighted. When Emily is around, everything goes as it should.'

M. Bernard scowled at this allusion to the way things were going, but she did not mind. It was just as well to let him know she was not pleased.

When she and the abbé were in the car again, and driving back to town, he said abruptly, 'What an unpleasant man.'

Oddly, she knew without asking to whom he referred. 'M. Gastion? Yes, he is, isn't he? He looks at you in a peculiar way — as if he knew everything about you, even all those dark things you never quite know about yourself.'

'As if he saw straight through, to that hiding man he was talking about,' the abbé said.

7

But he is a very fine cat,
a very fine cat indeed.
—Samuel Johnson

It was not quite spring yet, a delicious time of year to be in Paris, Emily thought. The city was one of her favorites. Rome had its sense of timelessness, and London was no doubt the most civilized city in the world, but Paris — all that noise and confusion and color, blurring together like an impressionist's painting. And how striking the contrast between the vibrant city and this walled garden with its early flowers abloom and the ivy that softened the noises from the street beyond the wall.

'And the food,' she said aloud. 'I'll bet even for a cat the eating is superb.'

She reached down to stroke the great black cat at her feet. He stirred slightly, his purring a deep rumbling sound and rubbed against her leg.

They had met in the garden yesterday, soon after she had arrived, the cat jumping down from the garden wall to greet her. She had forgotten last night at dinner to ask the cat's name, and had not seen him again until this afternoon. He was certainly a friendly beast.

'Are you talking to yourself, darling?' a voice called from inside. Marge Dawson appeared in the open doorway. Marge, an old school girlfriend in whose house Emily was staying, was one of those women who somehow always seem too large for their surroundings. She dwarfed the rooms in her diminutive townhouse, and now the garden, which had seemed spacious enough a moment before, shrank noticeably.

'I was just talking to your cat.'

'Now that's a peculiar thing to say, since we have no cat, and never would have. Michael can't tolerate them, he says they make him itch.'

'Well, you certainly have one regardless. Look, right here — oh, it's gone.' The cat was not where it had been. It seemed to have disappeared into thin air.

'Well, he was here, right at my feet. And he was here last evening when I came out, so I just naturally assumed he was yours. A big black thing, the size of a dog, and with a bad paw, it looked like he'd been in a devil of a scrap.'

'For all I care, he could have six bad paws, and he still wouldn't be ours, nor have I ever seen him,' Marge said. 'And if Michael saw him, he'd probably damage another paw. Come inside, pet, and let's have a drink before he comes down. He disapproves of martinis, and you are my excuse for having one.'

Emily glanced back once as they went into the house and caught a glimpse of something black moving through the shrubbery.

So, the cat knew enough to avoid the Dawsons.

'Clever cat,' she thought, and smiled to think that Parisian cats might be a little more sophisticated than others.

They had drinks in the parlor and talked of old school acquaintances and the shows Emily had seen in New York, and the seemingly endless difficulties the Paris Opera was having with the government. Michael, Marge's husband, came down, scowled at his wife's martini, and began to lecture Emily on architectural trends. Michael was an architect.

He was still lecturing on architectural trends at the dinner table. On his right was the French stage actress, Daphne DeLong. She was very beautiful and very successful, although her rivals were inclined to say, 'She can't act at all, you know, it's those eyes of hers.'

Just now she had those eyes, great luminous orbs, glued to Michael's and she responded to his lengthy explanations of architectural styles with comments like, 'How fascinating,' and, 'Isn't that exciting.'

'Michael, dear, stop boring Daphne with architecture,' Marge said across the table. They had finished eating — 'a really superb dinner,' Emily had exclaimed — and were having coffee. They were eight, and the drawing room was too small to seat that many comfortably, so they had lingered at the table for coffee.

Besides the Dawsons, Daphne and Emily, there were a M. Boulez, a Doctor Pritchard, and a Lord and Lady Van Cleve, who had just recently come over from London.

'Emily, darling,' Marge said, leaning down the table, 'M. Boulez is a writer, just like Elliot.'

M. Boulez looked a bit flustered at being singled out, and he murmured, 'I've only done a book or two. No international bestsellers, I'm afraid.'

'My brother-in-law hasn't done that much yet.'

'M. Boulez is a world famous authority on the occult and black magic,' Marge added.

'Not world famous, certainly,' M. Boulez objected.

'And,' Marge went on undaunted, 'he tells me the house that Elliot and Irene inherited is a positive hotbed of ghosts and ghouls.'

'Heavens,' Emily said, amused at M. Boulez' flustered manner. 'Should I practice an exorcism when I arrive?'

'I never said ghosts,' M. Boulez said in

his soft, almost feminine voice. 'I'm afraid I know almost nothing of the house's recent history, but it is rather infamous. It has a notoriously evil past.'

'And you said that things like that don't just go away, they hang around,' Marge said.

He smiled at her choice of expression. 'What I said is that evil may sometimes linger, as an unseen presence. I wondered if your sister and her husband had detected anything? Nothing concrete, that is, just a feeling of evil or unhappiness about the place?'

'I haven't been there myself, of course,' Emily said thoughtfully. 'Irene's letters when she first arrived certainly indicated that she wasn't happy, but that might not mean anything. She's something of a baby, and she didn't want to leave New York, so she would have been unhappy wherever they went.'

'Or it might be those evil spirits hanging around,' Marge said.

'But that's practically the same thing as saying there are ghosts and witches and the like,' Daphne said, her blue eyes wide and frightened looking. It was a look that had made perhaps a million young men want to rush to protect her.

Lady Agatha van Cleve, who loathed actresses, smiled wryly. 'I doubt Miss Hastings believes in witches and evil spirits. Americans are notoriously practical people.'

'I don't know that I would put it quite like that,' Emily said. 'I know nothing about ghosts, but as for witches, or evil, it's silly to say they don't exist. People have been burned because they were witches, haven't they, and there are still people who claim to be. And we can read about all sorts of evil in the daily newspaper.'

'Yes, yes,' Michael agreed, 'but that's all natural. I think Lady Agatha was referring to the supernatural. None of us believes in that, except old Boulez here, and I think it's just book material for him.'

'But the supernatural, after all, is only something for which we have not yet uncovered the natural laws, is it not?' Emily said.

'I don't follow that,' Daphne murmured.

M. Boulez smiled his pleasure at Emily and nodded his head. 'What Miss Hastings means is, much of what we now take for granted would have seemed supernatural once, because it was outside the province of the then-known natural laws. Our telephones, our televisions, our automobiles, even, and airplanes, would all have seemed like magic a century or two ago. The magic that witches once used has frequently been absorbed into accepted science.

'As an instance, English witches once used a type of mold to heal various ailments, and this was laughed at, but doctors today swear by penicillin, which is produced from a mold. Witch doctors once amused explorers with the use of a certain drug to heal illnesses of the soul, until someone investigated and found the ancestor of the modern day tranquilizer. The healings that resulted from these applications were magic in their day because the scientific properties were unknown. Today they are quite natural to us. Fifty years from the now the magic of clairvoyance or telepathy may seem commonplace because we will have discovered the laws that govern them.'

'One can't help thinking of the power of suggestion, too,' Doctor Pritchard said. 'A great deal of what was considered magic must have been at least in part the result of that. Every doctor today is aware of the placebo effect in treating a patient.'

The conversation had gotten too weighty for Daphne, and she brought it once more back to her level.

'But Miss Hastings,' she said, 'do you mean you think there are actual evil spirits that can overcome us?'

Emily smiled and said, 'I believe there is evil, in many forms, but I think evil as an influence exists as a possibility in our lives, which can be real for us only if we accept it and permit it to act in us, through us.'

Lord van Cleve, who had been silent until now, said, 'Doesn't that rather negate the existence of an omnipotent God?'

'I don't think so,' Emily said thoughtfully. 'Not even an all-powerful God could make us perfect without giving us the power of selection. Unless we were free to choose between good and evil, we would not be good, we would only be automatons. Good and evil exist so that we may choose between them.'

Daphne gave a little gasp and put her hand to her throat. 'Oh, there's something at the window,' she said.

They all looked in that direction. 'I don't see anything,' Marge said. The light within and the darkness without made a black mirror of the French windows. Nothing could be seen but their own reflections.

'I saw a pair of eyes, peeking in,' Daphne said. 'They looked . . . evil.'

'It's all this talk about hobgoblins,' Michael said. He did not much care for any conversation that strayed from the subject of architecture.

'Michael, do go see if there is anyone in the garden,' Marge said.

The cat, Emily thought, but did not say so.

'And if there are any prowlers out there,' Marge called after her husband, 'don't tackle them yourself. Remember your bad back. Come in here and we'll call the police.'

Michael found no prowlers in the garden, however, and when he came back, he diverted the conversation back to architecture.

* * *

Emily had forgotten all about the cat when, during the night, she was awakened by a scratching noise. At first she could not locate it, but finally she realized it was coming from the direction of the window.

Hardly knowing what to expect, she slipped from the bed and crossed the cool tile floor to draw the curtains aside. The black cat was outside, his considerable bulk practically filling the window. As she looked out, he scratched at the casement, plainly indicating that he wanted to come inside. It had begun to rain, and at the sight of Emily, he began to meow. He looked utterly pathetic out there in the weather, pleading to be let in.

'Oh, dear heart,' Emily said, unlocking the window and sliding it open, 'you heard what Marge said earlier today. If Michael found you in my room, he might break both your paws, and mine in the bargain.'

The animal seemed quite undaunted at that prospect. He stepped smartly inside and with a whir like an electric motor, began to purr and rub against her.

She was too softhearted to thrust him back into the inclement night. 'All right,' she said in a whisper. 'You can sleep in here, but I hope you're an early riser, and that,' she pointed at the open window, 'is the way out, before Marge comes around, okay?'

He was certainly pleased at being with her. She could not remember ever knowing a more affectionate animal. In bed, he literally seemed to embrace her, putting his paws about her neck and nestling his cool nose against her throat. She thought it an unnatural pose for a cat, and she worried that his weight on her would probably keep her awake, but it did not. His purr was a soothing rumble, and she fell asleep almost at once.

She woke to a throbbing, grinding pain

that radiated out from her throat, up into her head, and down through all of her body. She felt like her limbs were made of lead. She opened her eyes, but the glare of light hurt them, and she closed them immediately, giving a little moan. At once there was a hand on her forehead.

'Don't try to move,' Marge said, as if from a great distance. 'Try to rest. You'll feel better later.'

Emily let herself sink back into the softness of the pillow. Her weight seemed to be bearing her back and down, down, down.

'She must have caught a chill from leaving the window open,' Marge said to someone. 'It hardly seems that cold out. The poor dear, she's burning up with fever.'

★ ★ ★

Irene read the letter over again quickly, and with an unhappy sigh, folded it and put it into her purse.

'She isn't coming,' she said flatly. 'She's been sick in bed for almost two weeks, and now her time has run short and she has to be back in New York. So, she's sorry, and she'll be back to see us in a month or so.'

Elliot, across the table from her at the café, was equally disappointed. 'That's too bad,' he said, stirring his now cold coffee. 'There must be something going around.'

'Have you been to see M. Bernard?' she asked.

'I saw the housekeeper. She says his condition is no better. Still running a high fever. Too weak even to sit up. She thinks he should be in the hospital.'

'And in the meantime, we pay a crew of workmen to pile garbage in little heaps, and the little heaps into big heaps.'

'Not entirely. Thank God for M. Gastion. I've let him have a free hand, and he's done rather a nice job. He said again today he would take charge of the project, if we wanted.'

Irene glanced away. She knew he wanted to have that responsibility off his own shoulders, and that he would be happy to give the job to M. Gastion, were it not for her reservations.

Worst of all, she could not but think she was being unreasonable. She had no specific reason to dislike M. Gastion as she did, but the truth was, she could hardly bear to lay eyes upon the man.

'He's in the book business,' Elliot said. 'He seems to know everyone in publishing. He's rather hinted he might look at some of my work and see if he could give me any help.'

'Darling, I can't help it. I just don't like the man. I'm frightened of him, and I know it's silly, but that's the way it is. I could never come up to the house to stay while he's there.'

Elliot let the subject drop, and stirred his coffee again.

8

Will you, I pray,
demand that demi-devil
Why he hath thus ensnar'd
my soul and body?
—William Shakespeare

Irene was in the dining room of the hotel the following morning when the proprietress, a nervous little hen of a woman, came bustling in from her own apartment in the rear.

'Ah, Madame, I am glad to see you,' she said, wiping her hands on her apron. She was out of breath, as if she had been hurrying. 'I shall not be able to serve you lunch today. I am called away.'

Irene was in the habit of having her lunch at the hotel, but the food was no more than mediocre, and she did not much mind having to go elsewhere. 'It's quite all right,' she said.

After a pause, the proprietress volunteered

the information that Irene had not asked for. 'It's my mother,' she said.

'I hope it's nothing serious.'

'Life is so hard,' the woman said, wringing her hands. 'And my mother, ah, if only she were not so difficult. She is eighty, you understand, and she lives at a distance. Not that she isn't welcome here, you understand — all these rooms, we would not be crowded, would we? But no, she wants to stay by herself. And now she is sick, and a neighbor calls me and says she is crying for me, and I must come to her, and my husband is away today, so there is nothing I can do but leave the hotel unattended. Life is a plague, is it not?'

'I am so sorry,' Irene said. 'If I can help . . . perhaps I can keep an eye on things here?'

'Oh, that is kind, thank you, but I doubt that anyone will come today for a room, and if someone comes for lunch, perhaps you will just tell them we are closed for the day.'

'Of course.' Irene got up to leave, but the proprietress motioned her to remain.

'Please, I do not mean the room is

closed to you. Make yourself at home, I beg you.' She bustled back out again, and Irene went back to writing letters to friends in the States.

Less than an hour later, the proprietress again came through, this time dressed in a street dress and a frayed coat, and carrying a small satchel. They exchanged goodbyes, as if she might be leaving for days, and then Irene was alone in the room once more. For all she knew, she might be alone in the hotel. There had been only one other guest of late, an Englishman, and he had gone yesterday.

She finished her letters and prepared the last of them for mailing. There was a restaurant near the post office, and it was not long until lunchtime. She would stroll in that direction and mail her letters, and then have something to eat. Afterward, she would go by the house.

Or perhaps not. Elliot would not be pleased to see her, and she would not be pleased, she was certain, to see how the work was going. In any case, she was sure to encounter M. Gastion if she went to the house.

She was quite surprised, then, to see M. Gastion when she stepped to the sidewalk a little later. He was passing slowly by, and as he did not seem to have seen her emerging from the hotel, she deliberately shrank back into its shadows, hoping to avoid a meeting.

Suddenly he came to a stop and clapped one hand over his heart. With a cry, he sank to his knees on the pavement. As Irene watched in horror, he fell flat upon the ground.

He had been stricken ill, and there was nothing that she could do but go to him and see if she could help. She hadn't a hard enough heart to allow her to remain where she was and watch the man die.

He looked pale, and might even have been dead, except he opened his mouth and gasped for breath. She knelt down, looking around for assistance, but the street appeared deserted. She was at a loss what to do, when he opened his eyes and saw her.

'Ah, Madame l'Américaine,' he gasped, 'help me inside, I beg you.'

'But I don't think I can,' she stammered,

sure that she could never manage to carry him or drag him inside.

'Help me,' he begged. He struggled to get to his feet. He leaned heavily upon her, but with their combined efforts they managed to get him into the hotel dining room, where he sank weakly into one of the chairs.

'Let me get you some water,' she said.

'No — there are some tablets in my left-hand pocket. Get me one of those, please.'

She found the pills in a case and gave him one, which he swallowed.

'It's my heart,' he whispered. 'It does not often trouble me, but when it does, it can be severe. I might have died today had it not been for your kind assistance.'

'I'm only grateful I was nearby at the time.'

He closed his eyes and she saw he wanted to rest. She moved quietly about the room, restless and yet not wishing to be rude and simply leave him alone. The curtains were open. A large tree sheltered the windows, so that the room was dim and gloomy, but she could appreciate that in the hot weather it might be cool.

'I am intruding,' M. Gastion said.

He looked better now and his voice was steady. She realized for the first time that he had an odd way of looking at a person. He seemed to be looking not at but through you, at something beyond.

Meeting his gaze, as intimate as ever, she found her pity leaving her, and again she was filled with dislike for the man.

'Anyone would have done the same,' she said indifferently.

He sensed at once the change in her manner, and said, 'I think I should leave you now.'

He got up from his chair, but he had taken no more than two steps before he groaned and stumbled, and once again went to his knees. She sprang to help him, and as she did so, she felt a wave of guilt at her rudeness to a man who was obviously quite ill.

'I'm sorry.' She helped him back to the chair. 'Please, stay as long as you like. Can I get you anything? I'm sure the proprietress will not mind if I bring you some brandy.'

'Nothing. Only let me sit here for a little while.'

'As long as you like,' she said, helpless and conscience stricken. 'I'll stay here with you until you are better.'

He closed his eyes again, and thinking he would rest, she went to another chair and sat in it, putting one hand to her temples. She felt oddly disturbed. Her heart was beating uncommonly fast, and the room had become warm and very close, although the day outside had been cool.

After a time, he asked, 'Can you really dislike me so much?'

'What difference can it make, whether I like you or not?'

He gave a great sigh that frightened her because she thought for a moment he was having another attack. 'If you knew how lonely and unhappy my life has been,' he said, 'you would have a little pity on an old man.'

There was something pathetically moving in his voice, so that she did indeed feel a wrench of pity in her heart. She felt that she had been unnecessarily cold toward the man, for no valid reason.

'You think I am being selfish in butting into your lives,' he went on, without waiting for a reply. 'You will not give me credit for truly wanting to help. Do you think I do not long for your approval, for your friendship? But how am I to have it, if you will not let me earn it?'

She sat in silence, listening. There was something different about his voice, something silken and seductive. She did not know why, but his words, soft and low, made her pulse quicken.

'I disgust you, I know,' he said. 'I can see it in your eyes when you look at me.'

'No,' she said, but she knew her denial sounded insincere.

'It breaks my heart that you feel so toward me. You are good and pure, I can see that, and it makes me feel unclean to think of your dislike for me. I feel that I must be less than human.'

She had not meant to look at him and yet against her conscious intention, she did so. She was surprised to see he looked quite different. His eyes had a new expression in them that she had not seen before. They were tender, glistening with tears, but with some strange invitation, too. His mouth trembled as he returned her gaze.

'You are so beautiful.' He was speaking now in little more than a whisper, and yet his words seemed to echo in her mind, not so much as if she heard them, but rather as if she felt them within her.

'Beautiful, and a little weary of the world, I saw that when I first laid eyes on you. Yours is not merely an outward beauty, either, but something that glows from within. I look at you and I see all the world, all the history of man. I see in your eyes what men have seen in the *Mona Lisa*, that knowledge of the secret mysteries of life, and of love.'

She was intoxicated by the sound of his words. They stirred something within her, some dark part of her soul that moved restlessly and seemed to be slowly awakening from a deep slumber.

'You are older than time, and as young as tomorrow,' his voice droned on. 'You have died before, and learned the secrets of death, and lived again. You are Helen of Troy, and Cleopatra, and Saint Anne, and you and I have been together through all history.'

He began to speak then of himself, and he spoke openly, frankly, with no fear of shocking her. Indeed, she was not shocked, although he spoke of things not commonly discussed between a man and a woman who were only casually acquainted. He painted a portrait for her, a portrait of himself, and it quickly began to take form before her eyes, as clearly as if it were painted with oil paints upon canvas.

She saw him as he truly was: cruel and indifferent, indolent and passionate. He was sensual and at the same time a cold man. In his mind dwelt unnatural knowledge, and crimes for which he bore no guilt, and lusts that belonged more to the lower animals than to man.

Yet for all of that, she saw that he was *man*, a multitude of men throughout the ages of history. He made himself one with an army of spirits that paraded before her, all linked in their evil, in their thirst for dark knowledge. He was all the evil that had ever been. He was every wicked man who had ever lived.

His words traced a pattern on her soul. She was filled with a strange sense of sin and decadence, and of passion. She wondered what was happening to her, but she was powerless to resist.

9

*What potions have I drunk
of siren tears,
Distill'd from limbecks
foul as hell within.*
—William Shakespeare

Irene was disgusted and yet fascinated. His eyes held hers so that she could not look away, and his voice seemed actually to reflect the very beating of her heart. She had a peculiar languorous feeling. She might almost have been asleep. Her limbs were weightless, and she doubted her ability to move them at all.

He ceased speaking finally, and still she sat silent and motionless, as if she were waiting. She saw him rise from his chair and wondered almost unconcernedly what he was going to do next. He had apparently recovered completely from his earlier attack.

A bowl, a cheap ceramic thing, sat on

the table near her. He took something from his pocket and dropped this into the bowl. He did nothing more than gesture above the bowl with his hands, but suddenly a low flame sprang to life in the bottom of the dish. A thick odor filled the room. Irene inhaled it and found it pungent and repulsive. She coughed. She wanted to beg him to take it away, but she could not find her voice.

He lifted the bowl in his two hands and held it toward her. 'Look,' he said. 'Look into the bowl.'

She did not hesitate, but did as he had commanded. The blue fire that had burned within it was not a fire at all. It was something strangely alive, something that writhed eerily, like blue serpents.

'Breathe,' he ordered her. A sudden darkness came over her, and she trembled violently. She tried to scream, but no sound came from her throat. She had a sensation of spinning about, head over heels, as if she were moving through the air, traveling at a terrible speed, and she was terrified. It was like being caught up in a hurricane.

'Open your eyes,' he said finally.

She opened her eyes and looked about. It was night, but not the calm restful night she had known often in the past. This was a troublesome darkness, filled with vague whispering sounds, like the passing of giant birds overhead. Lights flickered here and there, like fireflies, and she saw that they stood on a great wasteland of rocks and cliffs and twisted trees. She knew that M. Gastion held her hand, and she was glad for its feel. It was as if she had traveled to the land of every childish nightmare, of every troubled sleep.

They were not alone in this darkness, for the air about them was filled with shadows, forms that swept close and then drifted back, like the waves breaking upon the shore, and came again, closer.

Suddenly, all was still, and an eerie green light pierced the darkness. One tree, twisted and wasted, stood before them. It appeared to have suffered great pain and torment, as if it were human, or more than human. Its tortured branches were lifted like the arms of a giant, in anguish.

She watched, sick with fear, and the tree came to life, the branches became arms, the roots clinging to the earth became feet. It was brutish and horrible, with horns and a shaggy beard, and hairy legs that ended in hoofs. The face was human and yet not human, grotesque with lust and cruelty, and yet somehow wildly appealing. The lecherous eyes caressed her, and she could almost feel their touch.

The creature shimmered and seemed to melt, and became altogether a man, a beautiful young man. He was Michelangelo's Adam, the Donatello David. He was Salome's Iokanaan, with the body whiter than 'the breast of the moon when she lies on the breast of the sea.' He was sublime, full of majesty, and she wanted to touch him, to sink into the abyss of his eyes. In his smile was all the sorrow of the world, and all the wickedness.

'Do not be afraid,' M. Gastion said. 'I have an art for which all things are possible. It controls the elements and the stars and the planets. I can make the moon fall blood red from the sky, and the dead rise up and speak with the night wind. Heaven and Hell obey me. I am all that is, and has been, and will be. Life and death are in my right and left hands, and immortality is my province.'

Before her, the youth beckoned, and she felt once more something dark and unknown stir within her.

At last she spoke. In a whisper, she said, 'Show me.' She did not know for what she asked. Some part of her mind knew that something horrible was upon her, and it beat like an imprisoned bird with helpless fluttering against the cage that held it, but she knew it was too late now to draw back, that with her words she had somehow sealed a bargain between them.

The youth disappeared into a cloud, and once again a throng of spirits surrounded her. They took form now, and she saw all of the foul beasts and legendary monsters that man had ever fancied. They defied description. They crept and crawled and leapt. They were winged, and slimy, and scaly, and some were nearly human, but they were the condemned of Dante's Inferno, and when they laughed it was like the knell of death.

A woman approached her, holding out a chalice of wine. Irene took it, and drank, and it was blood that spilled from the corners of her mouth, staining her blouse.

A sudden fire burned in her veins, and she could almost feel her soul fleeing, and another taking its place. She knew all that was wicked and evil and obscene. Before her eyes a hideous festival of lust was taking place, and she was a part of it. It was indescribably horrible, and yet she responded to it as a violin responds to the bow that plays upon its strings. Beside her, M. Gastion laughed with derision.

'You will be all right now,' he said, and suddenly his voice was natural and they were again in the dining room of the hotel. She looked around, frightened. Everything was as it had been before.

She remembered her dream then, and remembered that this man had been in it, and she was seized with an awful shame. Her cheeks burned and she put her face in her hands and began to cry.

'Please leave me,' she sobbed. 'Go away.'

He smiled, and nodded his head. She closed her eyes briefly, and when she looked up he was gone, although she had not heard him leave.

A moment later she heard a sound on the street. She was afraid he had come back and she jumped to her feet, prepared to flee from him into the village rather than remain alone with him again, but it was the proprietress who came in, looking flushed and out of breath.

'It's terrible,' she panted, banging her satchel down upon a table. 'The jokes they play these days, on a woman of my advanced years. An hour's train ride there and an hour's train ride back, and all for a joke.'

'Is your mother all right?' Irene asked mechanically, making an effort to regain her composure.

'There was nothing at all wrong with her,' the woman said with an angry snort. 'It was a practical joke. Has anyone been in?'

'No, no one.' The lie slipped out unbidden. She was surprised to have said it, and her cheeks colored.

The proprietress sniffed the air. 'What's that awful smell? Have you had lunch?'

Irene felt an overwhelming urge to be alone. 'Yes, I ate out,' she said, starting toward the stairs that would take her up to her room.

'You've forgotten your letters.'

The letters Irene had written earlier were still lying on the table by her handbag, waiting to be posted. It felt a century ago that she had started out to mail them.

'Oh, you've hurt yourself,' the landlady cried.

Irene looked down. To her horror she saw her blouse was stained with blood. She remembered in a vivid flash of memory the chalice of her hallucination, from which she had drunk wine that had turned to blood. She gave a little gasp of anguish.

On an impulse she seized the letters she had written and began to tear them to shreds. She threw the scraps into the waste receptacle by the stairs and, without a word to the astonished proprietress, she ran up the stairs to her room.

10

O, woe is me,
To have seen what I have seen,
see what I see!
—William Shakespeare

Irene had managed very nearly to persuade herself that M. Gastion's visit had been altogether innocent and that she had let her imagination run away with her. She had been under a strain, after all, and everything was so strange here and foreign to her, it was not surprising that she should have funny dreams.

She had decided that she would mention quite casually to Elliot that M. Gastion had been by. 'Not,' she would add quickly, 'to pay a visit. He got sick as he was going by, and I made him come in and sit a while.'

When Elliot came in late that afternoon, however, when he kissed her and she saw his simple, trusting love for her in his eyes, she felt embarrassed and oddly guilty. The words she had intended to speak stuck in her throat, and she let the opportunity of speaking them pass by, and after a while, it would have been awkward to bring them up. Elliot would surely wonder why she had not mentioned them at once.

It was Elliot, in fact, who, much later in the evening, brought up the subject. 'M. Gastion was by,' he said when they were preparing for bed. 'He asked again about taking charge of the restoration, and he asked me if I would bring the matter up with you once more. He seemed to think you might have changed your mind. Of course, I told him it was only a waste of time, that when you made your mind up to something, it stayed made up.'

Irene was seated at the little dressing table, applying cream to her face. She paused in her ministrations and looked into her own frightened eyes in the mirror. She fancied it was not her own face there, so pale and drawn, but the face of a stranger. For a moment she thought she saw M. Gastion, standing just behind her in the glass, grinning. He reached a hand toward her bare shoulder, and she gave an involuntary shudder, but it was only her imagination. When she looked again, there was no one present but Elliot, watching her curiously from the bed.

'Are you all right?' he asked.

'Yes, of course,' she said, 'why shouldn't I be?' She dabbed furiously at her face with the cream.

'You looked so, I don't know exactly. Stricken, I suppose.'

'I was . . . I was thinking of the landlady. She had a terrible practical joke played upon her today. Someone called to say her mother was sick, and she made a two hour trip there and back, to discover it was only a prank.'

She removed the cream with a towel and put it aside. 'Perhaps you've been right about M. Gastion,' she said, coming to bed. 'M. Bernard seems to be getting no better, and the work has come to a virtual standstill. Perhaps it would be foolish to continue to refuse M. Gastion's offer.'

Elliot looked both surprised and relieved.

'Yes, that's true,' he said. 'After all, he may be an agent of divine providence.'

She said nothing in reply to that, although she looked at him for a long moment before turning out the light.

They made love, and Elliot was surprised and delighted by the intensity of his wife's ardor.

★　★　★

They moved the following day into the house in the country. It seemed to Irene that already much had been accomplished since her last visit, which must be credited to Gastion's efforts. They had been marking time, waiting for M. Bernard to recover, but even before he took sick the work had been going badly. Now there was a distinct air of decisiveness that was reassuring. All of the men were hard at work and one could almost watch the results of their labors taking shape.

Before, the great hall had been filled with debris that almost accumulated faster than it could be carried out, but now it was clean and already beginning to show the grandeur it had only hinted at before.

'It's really looking marvelous,' Irene said. 'What's that?'

Two men struggled up from the cellars, carrying between them what appeared to be an immense pane of dirty glass.

Elliot said. 'It's a glass painting.'

'A glass painting?'

'A picture painted on glass. They were very popular at one time, apparently. M. Gastion says this one used to hang over the fireplace there.'

The painting was of such an immense size that there was some difficulty in getting it from the corridor into the hall.

'I think we'll have to remove part of the woodwork,' Elliot said. 'Let it rest there for now.'

The men propped the painting against the wall and went back to the cellars. Irene walked around to where she could see the painting, and gave a little shudder of disgust.

'Oh, it's awful,' she cried. 'It's — it's obscene.'

The painting was filthy, so that it took a moment of study to make out the subject matter, and then one saw it only darkly. It was a painting of a man, dressed in black, with shining silver buttons, and silver buckles on his shoes. He pushed his way through a thick tangle of brush and over his shoulder, as carelessly as if she were a sack of flour, he carried a woman's body.

Against the pink of her flesh could be seen the crimson slashes of blood where the brambles had torn her flesh. Her head hung down, her eyes were closed as if she were dead or fainting and one hand trailed limply through the grass.

The effect of the painting, even in its dulled state, was hideous and grotesque. Irene felt a wave of nausea. Something about it recalled to her the visions she had experienced the day before under M. Gastion's influence.

'You can't mean to hang this in the hall,' she said.

'M. Gastion says that's where it belongs, and that it's a masterpiece.'

'It's awful.'

'Let's see what it looks like cleaned up.

It is grotesque, I'll admit, but if you don't take it seriously, it has its humorous aspects. Remember Helen Winston used to tell everybody she was a witch. No one took her seriously, but it was amusing. This could be the same thing.'

Irene did not think she could ever regard this painting as amusing, but she let the subject end there and went to the rooms in which they would be living while the restoration continued.

They were pleasant rooms in the rear of the second floor, so that she had a view of the woods and the old mill. She did not immediately put herself to unpacking, but went instead to the window seat and stared out at the view. Despite its loveliness, she would have given anything in the world to have it traded for the skyline of Manhattan. She longed to be gone from here, to be home. She felt inexpressibly sad, and tears welled up in her eyes, blurring the scene outside the window.

She felt so ashamed of herself. It was her nature to be truthful, and she had always been open and frank with Elliot. Several times she had come close to telling him about her visit from M. Gastion, but something had seemed to impel her, against her nature, to continue to conceal that from him, and now she knew she hadn't the courage to tell him.

There was a sound at the door, and she gave a terrified cry and leapt to her feet. She thought for an instant that it was M. Gastion, and her eyes were wide with terror as the door opened, but it was her husband.

'Hello, you look a fright,' he said, regarding her curiously.

She ran into his arms. She felt physically weak, and for a moment she could only cling to him and give herself up to tears.

Although he was not usually sensitive to feminine emotions, Elliot was a gentle man. He held her tenderly and let her vent her emotions.

At last she sobbed, 'Elliot, darling, take me away from here, please.'

He laughed softly, thinking he understood. His wife was homesick. It was as simple as that. She had seemed preoccupied. He was relieved to know it was nothing serious after all.

'Darling, we can't just go away, not in the midst of all this work.'

'I want to go home.'

'But this is our home. It would mean financial disaster for us to try to go back now.'

'I have money.'

'We've been through all that. Anyway, there's no reason for us to go back. The renovations are well under way, and in a few weeks we'll be able to live like a king and a queen here. We can have the sort of life I've always wanted for us.'

She listened with diminishing sobs. He would never agree to live on her money, and she could see that he was right as far as the house was concerned. Even if she tried to explain, if she told him what had happened, he would only think she was being foolish.

She freed herself from his embrace and dried her eyes with a handkerchief. Elliot was pleased to see she had recovered her composure.

'M. Gastion has arrived. He's going to outline his plans for the rest of the work.

Do you want to join us?'

She had been looking down, but now her head jerked up and there was an odd expression in her eyes. He might almost have thought she was terrified.

It was only an instant, though, and then it was gone, and she was cool and collected once more. 'No,' she said softly. 'I think I will take care of unpacking.'

'Don't work too hard. We have all the time in the world.'

'Have we?' She did not wait for an answer. 'Has M. Gastion moved into the house, then?'

'Yes. His room is the far-east one, on this floor. I forgot, he said to be sure to tell you which it was, in case you wanted him for anything.'

She turned her back on him and was silent. Elliot felt uncomfortable, as if there were something he ought to be doing, and could not remember. 'Well, I'll go down to him, then.'

He started from the room, but she spoke his name and he turned back.

She said, 'If anything should happen to me here, the fault will be yours.'

'What could happen to you here, of all places? After Manhattan, I should think you'd feel quite safe here. I'll bet there isn't a mugger for two hundred miles.'

He had meant to make a joke of whatever was bothering her, but she turned her back on him again.

He hesitated for a moment longer. He remembered that she had been afraid of M. Gastion when they had first met the man, and now M. Gastion had moved into the house with them. He wondered if that could have anything to do with his wife's odd mood.

Yet it was she who had made the decision to have M. Gastion help them, and to let him move into the house. Frankly, he had been more than a little surprised by the decision, but Irene would surely not have suggested that if she had been still afraid of him.

He shrugged and went out, closing the door gently. He thought, not for the first time, that women were difficult to understand.

11

*I had most need of blessing,
and 'Amen'
Stuck in my throat.*
—William Shakespeare

Irene stayed in her room during the day, and so managed to avoid the sight of M. Gastion. She could not explain this, even to herself. She knew that with him living in the house she must sooner or later, meet him again; but she could not bear the thought of seeing him, and her thoughts did not go beyond the immediate moment.

When time came to go out for dinner, as they were not yet set up to do any real cooking, Elliot came up to get her.

'I'm sorry, darling,' she said, 'I have a splitting headache. Do you mind if I just stay here?'

'You aren't coming down with something, are you?' he asked, worried because she really did look a little under the weather.

To his surprise, she only laughed and shook her head, but her laugh was completely without mirth, and a moment later she threw herself across the bed in an attitude of anguish. He went to dinner with M. Gastion, and brought her back a cold supper.

Except that he was a bit concerned for her, Elliot was in a buoyant mood. He was excited with the way the work was progressing under Gastion's guidance.

Irene lay for most of the night and listened to her husband's untroubled sleep. She wondered grimly if she would ever sleep so easily again — she who had never, not once in her life, been troubled by insomnia. The truth was, she was afraid to sleep, afraid of what visions might come to her when she had crossed over into that realm of darkness and fantasy.

The next day she felt fatigued and highly wrought. She looked back upon her meeting with M. Gastion and felt sure it had been no accident. She was certain now that it was he who had pulled the prank on the hotel proprietress, and she was sure too his illness had been faked.

She was convinced he had somehow hypnotized her, but oddly, she no longer was angry. Before, she had felt an inexplicable loathing for him, but this emotion too had vanished. Although it dismayed her, she could not get the man from her thoughts. The things he had said to her, and the nightmarish visions he had inspired in her, seemed almost to have taken possession of her. It was as if some evil seed had been planted within her, and had begun to grow, sending its poisonous roots into everywhere.

Nothing distracted her. If she tried to read, she found herself seeing and hearing not the words in the book, but the words of M. Gastion. If she tried to look at the view from the window, she saw his image in the glass. Moment by moment, she felt his presence in the room with her.

She was frightened of the man, and yet her fear was without the physical repulsion she had known toward him in the past. She told herself that she did not want ever to see him again. At the same time, she felt an almost irresistible desire to go to him wherever he was. She was haunted by the knowledge that he was here, within the same house with her, his room but a few yards away.

She struggled against this fascination, but in her heart she was not entirely certain she wanted to resist. She wanted to be with him, and yet she was terrified of that knowledge. She felt that to yield to that temptation was to somehow seal her doom.

At last she knew she must turn to someone for help, and she remembered the abbé. She felt certain that gentle man would not laugh at her imagination, and if he could do nothing else for her, he might at least be able to persuade Elliot that it was best they go away from this place.

She stole from the house without a word to Elliot. Chiding herself that she was being foolish, she felt she hadn't a moment to lose, but when she got to the rectory, the abbé was out.

'It is the day he goes around to visit the sick,' the sister at the door explained. 'They are scattered about. I doubt that he will be back before evening, perhaps not until quite late.'

Irene's heart sank. Her last hope had been taken from her.

The sister asked, 'Would you like to come in and wait? Perhaps he will not be so very late.'

Irene hesitated, but she saw that she could not just disappear for the entire day without alarming Elliot. She shook her head and started away without a word.

'Shall I give the father a message?' the worried nun called after her.

Again, Irene hesitated. But what message could she leave for the abbé? And what good would it do? He would not be back until night, and it was now that she needed his help. What did she care about the future, when she could not endure the present? She went on without even a reply to the sister.

When she arrived back at the house, it was to receive yet another disappointment. One of the workmen came to tell her that Elliot was gone.

'He had to go into the city to make some purchases,' the man explained, 'and he said to tell you that if he was not back before nightfall, not to worry, as M.

Gastion would be here, so you wouldn't be alone in the house.'

She murmured some words of thanks and fled to the safety of her room, but there was no comfort to be found there. Fate was conspiring against her. She was helpless to resist the forces at work. She was like a drowning person, clinging to a rock. The waves dashed over her, drawing her inexorably into the turbulent waves.

She tried to pray, which she had not done since she was a child, but even the words of her childhood prayers eluded her and refused to come to her tongue.

Like a caged animal, she prowled her room, counting off the seconds. If only she could endure until Elliot returned home — but each second was an eternity. She paced and suffered, and felt surely an hour must have passed, only to discover, when she looked at her watch, that it was no more than a few minutes since she had last checked the time.

She locked the door to her room, only to rush back to it a moment later, unlock it, and fling the key through the open window.

At last she could struggle no longer. She threw open the door to her room and went into the hall. The house was silent. The workmen had left, and she knew she was alone in the house with her tormentor. Despite this fact, she crept along the corridor stealthily, as if afraid she might be seen. Her heart was pounding. With all her might, she tried to resist the urge drawing her along the hall, and yet she went. She stood trembling for a moment outside his door. Finally, she knocked.

He opened the door to her at once, not at all surprised to see her, and he said, 'I've been waiting for you to come.'

He ushered her into the room. She sat in a chair that he indicated. There was an acrid scent in the room. She had smelled the same scent in one of the visions she had suffered at their last meeting.

He said nothing. The silence grew long, and longer still. Her agony increased with each second, until at last she had to speak.

'What have you done to me?' she cried. 'Why won't you leave me alone?'

'If that is what you wish.' He seemed quite unperturbed. 'I shall do you no harm. Go, if you like, I shall not prevent your leaving.'

He gestured toward the door. She remained where she was, her heart thudding painfully. She did not want to go, despite her outburst. She felt physically drawn to him, and suddenly she ceased to resist. She felt divided against herself. She was frightened, and at the same time, elated.

He began to talk, as before, in that same low voice of his with its curious magic. At once her eyes closed, and her head fell back. She felt not so much as if she were listening, but rather as if she were being transported by his voice into another world, another life.

His words offered her a new existence, a life of freedom, of knowledge she had never dreamed of, of new sensations and new thrills. Beside this world of his, her existence with Elliot seemed pale indeed. How could she have endured the dullness of it so long, when her own loveliness lifted her above the common crowd? She was not meant to be a housewife, but an artist in the art of living, living such as ordinary mortals could never know nor understand. She had been a fool, denying everything within herself. She had lived as one woman, when in fact she was another one altogether, a woman of passion and excitement and blazing power.

Something soared within her, as if a new soul were born. 'Is this me?' she wondered, and as if she had spoken aloud, M. Gastion said, 'This is the you that has been hiding within all the while, waiting to come forth.'

The drowsiness passed away and at once she was alive to desires and feelings she had never known before. She sprang to her feet, her eyes flashing.

He stood, too, facing her. With a quick movement he seized her in his arms and kissed her. She did not try to resist. She welcomed his embrace, surrendered herself to him voluptuously. Her body burned with the ecstasy of his kiss.

'Haven't you something to say to me?' he asked after a while.

'I love you,' she whispered hoarsely.

'And what else?' His smile was mocking and confident, and she knew that he already knew her answer.

'I am your slave,' she murmured. She felt a sudden lightening of her spirit, as if a great burden had just been lifted from her.

He chuckled softly, and bent to kiss her once again.

12

Let's talk of graves.
—William Shakespeare

It troubled Elliot that he could not clearly define the change in his wife. That she had changed was obvious, and some of the results of the change were so blatant that he could hardly have remained unaware of them.

For one thing, there was her new passion. This part of their marriage had always been enjoyable to him, of course, but in the past it had been a relatively placid relationship, mildly exciting without ever being completely uninhibited. He was confident, even complacent, in their love, and so did not trouble himself. He knew that women expressed their love in different ways, and he put more importance on other aspects of their marriage.

These relations had changed dramatically, however. It would no longer be possible to describe Irene's role as passive or placid.

It was thrilling, her new desire for him. Yet at the same time there was something about it that troubled him. Had it not been the woman he loved and to whom he was married, he would almost have termed some of her behavior obscene.

It was exciting but when it was finished he could not say that he was altogether happy about it.

There were other changes as well that puzzled him. They went out one day into the woods, to examine the grounds. They were with M. Gastion, following a trail through the thickest part of the woods. At one point a bramble growing close to the path scratched Irene's bare arm.

'Damn,' she cried, seizing the arm and putting her mouth to the scratch.

Elliot had never heard his wife swear before, and the sound of that simple oath from her lips shocked him profoundly, but she seemed unaware of the reason for his surprise.

'What's wrong?' she asked sharply. 'Why are you looking at me so strangely?'

'I — I was afraid you'd hurt yourself,' he said.

'Let me see,' M. Gastion said, taking Irene's arm in his hand. He examined it. 'It is only a scratch. Do you want to go back to the house?'

Elliot was annoyed without knowing why. 'If it's only a scratch, as you say, there's no reason why we shouldn't go on. I have yet to have a real look around the property.'

'There's nothing more to see out this way but woods and bushes,' M. Gastion said. 'Perhaps, after all, we ought to go back. Sometimes little scratches like this one can be dangerous.'

'It's painful,' Irene declared, clasping her arm as if she had been sorely wounded.

The gesture did not ring true, however. Elliot had the impression she was play-acting in response to M. Gastion's remark. 'If you two want to go back, by all means do so,' he said. 'I want to see the rest of the property.' He went on, pushing through the undergrowth.

After a moment, Irene and M. Gastion

followed. Elliot had not gone far before he began to feel silly. It was not necessary to see the rest of the property this very day, considering that he and Irene would be living here the rest of their lives. He had been sharp with Irene, moreover, and he felt guilty for it, but he kept a stubborn silence, more because of his guilt than despite it, and he went on.

He paused suddenly, surprised to see through the trees before him the gleam of white marble, and a glimpse of a rusted iron railing.

'What's this?' he said aloud. The path widened abruptly into a clearing.

'It's a cemetery,' Irene said.

'I thought you said there was nothing out this way,' Elliot said to M. Gastion.

'I had forgotten.'

An iron railing surrounded the grave-yard, and directly before them stood an ironwork gate with rusted scrolls. On either side were stone pillars covered now with lichen and moss, and crumbling with the onslaught of time.

The gate was ajar, and without further hesitation, Elliot pushed it open.

It was a small cemetery and obviously had not been used in a long time. Elliot, looking around, said, 'This must be the de Garac graveyard.'

Irene shuddered slightly as he said this. She remembered what the abbé in town had told her of the family, and in this melancholy spot, permeated by the stench from the ancient tombs, those tales seemed all the more ominous. Something stirred faintly within her, an odd sense of remorse that eluded her when she tried to take hold of it.

'I don't like this place,' she said in a small voice. 'Let's leave.'

'There's no hurry,' Elliot said. 'Look, this mausoleum is the size of a house. It must be the tomb of the Marquises de Garac.'

The mausoleum stood off to itself on a small knoll. It was overgrown now with hedges and moss, and great patches of it had fallen away with age, but it remained impressive.

He went closer, the others trailing after him. The crypt was in the form of a Greek temple, with a marble portico.

Elliot saw the names of several of the de Garacs. Oddly, he noted that, while most tombs had both a birth date and a death date, these names had only one date inscribed after each of them.

'Perhaps,' M. Gastion said at his side, 'we should not disturb the dead.'

'I agree,' Irene said. 'This place is horrid.'

Elliot was unwilling to set aside his curiosity. 'Look here, the door's come loose on its hinges. We can go inside.'

'I don't think that would be wise,' M. Gastion said. Something in his voice gave the impression he was issuing a command. Elliot did not like being told what to do.

'I'll just have a look inside,' he said stubbornly, and went up the wide steps toward the entrance to the mausoleum. He seized the iron door and gave it a tug. As he did so, Irene gave a cry of alarm.

Elliot stepped back instinctively. It was this that saved his life. A great chunk of marble crashed down from above, landing on the very spot where he had been standing a second before. Fragments struck his leg and his outstretched arm.

He backed away, looking up at the place from which the marble had fallen. 'My God,' he said, 'I might have been killed.'

'I tried to warn you,' M. Gastion said with a dry smile. 'This place is crumbling into ruin. I am sure it is unsafe to go inside.'

'You may be right,' Elliot admitted reluctantly.

'Leave this place to me,' M. Gastion said, clapping a hand upon Elliot's shoulder. 'As I have told you before, everything is in my hands now.'

Again, Elliot had the impression of a double entendre, but while he was intelligent enough, he was not a witty man, and such subtleties confused him more than informed him.

He might yet have made an issue out of the business of the mausoleum, but when he glanced at his wife, he saw that she was as pale as the marble of the tomb. Chiding himself for being so thoughtless, he took her arm and began to lead the way back through the woods to the house.

13

And be
Procuress to the Lords of Hell.
—Alfred, Lord Tennyson

Every day, Irene felt the uncontrollable urge to visit M. Gastion in his rooms. Sometimes she went at night. She waited until Elliot was asleep, and then she would steal from their bed and hurry along the dark corridors.

Sometimes she stole to her assignations by daylight. She seemed to know instinctively, without the need of prearranged meetings, when he would be there and not on some work about the house.

He was always waiting to greet her in his cruel, indifferent manner. Each time she came, she paused outside his door. She did not know which fear was worse: that he might not be there, or that he would be. She hated the callousness with which he greeted her. She could not bear seeing him at all, but she could not bear not seeing him either. She stood outside his door, telling herself that she did not mean to go in this time, that she would turn about and go back to her own room, and end this thing now, but invariably she went in.

She did try to persuade herself not to go at all, but that was equally useless. She knew she was only pretending to herself. She did not want anything to interfere. If it seemed something might prevent their meeting, she was in a fit of irritation. She could not be happy — indeed, she did not feel that she was alive — except when she was in his company. When she was in his arms, and he kissed her, then and then alone did she know ecstasy. Nor did it seem to matter much that her ecstasy was mingled with loathing, or that she abhorred him even as she desired him.

When she looked into his pale eyes, and heard the low murmur of his voice, she forgot everything that had gone before. He seemed literally to transport her through time and space to magical realms. She traveled with him through the mysterious East. She saw the dawn upon ancient, desolate cities. Her nostrils were filled with the scent of myrrh and frankincense.

Sometimes it was as if he lifted a dark veil and revealed to her great secrets. She understood now, she who had never thirsted for knowledge, how men could barter their souls for learning. All of the kingdoms of darkness were spread at her feet.

She knew nothing of her master. He might have had no past, no life before this present moment. He seemed apart from human kind, but for all of this, she cared nothing.

'It need matter not at all who I am,' he told her when she questioned him, 'not where I have been, nor where I am going. I am here, and you are mine, and that is all you need to know.'

'Yes,' she said softly, and sank again into his arms.

Outwardly, her life proceeded with astonishing ordinariness. She found it easy to deceive Elliot, mostly because he had never distrusted her, and so believed whatever excuses she gave him. Once a lie would have been intolerable to her, but now she found that they rolled easily off her tongue.

Yet she could still feel shame for them. Sometimes when she had come back from a rendezvous with M. Gastion, and was lying beside Elliot, listening to the sound of his untroubled sleep, she was overcome with remorse.

It was out of her hands now, though, too far along for her to do anything. She blamed Elliot for everything. She had not wanted to come here at all, but he had insisted, and when they came, and she had sensed the aura of evil about the house, she had begged to go back to New York. And again, when M. Gastion had begun to wield his influence upon her, she had once more begged Elliot to take her away.

The blame was his for whatever had befallen them. She began even to hate him. She wondered how she could ever have loved him. He was ordinary looking and he was dull. He had kept her from enjoying the luxury she should have been able to enjoy, with his insistence that they live on his meager income. He had stifled her, never realizing all that was within her, awaiting expression.

In all that had happened between her and M. Gastion, however, Irene had somehow never questioned his feelings for her. She had taken it for granted that he loved her, and that it was his desire for her that had prompted him to take possession of her soul as he had. She was shocked almost beyond words, then, when he made mention of her sister, Emily.

'I want you to write to your sister,' he said one day without preamble, 'and insist that she come for a visit.'

'Emily? What on earth has she got to do with anything?'

'I want her here. That is all you need to know. Bring her here for me.'

She jumped to her feet, brushing off his hand, and stared at him in bewilderment. 'But why? What can you want with her?'

'There is no need to agitate yourself. It will do you no good. I want your sister here. If you can't accomplish what I ask, or won't, then I shall take that as a rejection, and I shall go away at once.'

Irene was suddenly seized with utter revulsion. The image of Emily, so sweet and good and kind, came to her mind, and it was followed by a vision of this monster corrupting Emily as he had corrupted her. She saw in that moment that, despite the horrible bond that tied her to him, he was loathsome, and she hated and feared him. For the first time in weeks she saw clearly. She saw Elliot, and his wonderful love for her, and she hated herself. She saw that she must free herself from this man's grasp. Not only her happiness, but her very soul, dangled in the balance, and not only her soul, but Emily's now as well.

'Go, then. I hate you. I wish I had never seen you. Nothing could give me more pleasure than that you should leave and never return.'

He was quite unperturbed. He rose slowly from the chaise and, going to the door, opened it for her. There was a hateful smile on his face as he gestured for her to leave.

Never in her life had she hated herself more, but when she went to pass him she was as horribly fascinated by him as she was horribly repelled. She wanted to be in his arms again. She trembled with the fervor of her desire. If he had made a single gesture to restrain her, she would have stayed and begged his forgiveness, but he let her pass, and when the door had closed after her and she was alone in the hall, she heard his mocking laughter from within.

She fled the house and went into the village. She had no destination in mind, and once in town she parked the car and hurried along the dusty streets, trying to collect her raging thoughts.

She came to the square of the town. It was a simple place, and yet uncommonly charming, with its splashing fountain and its graceful old church. She could take no pleasure in the scene, however. She sat on the stone bench and thought of Elliot and the utter trust he had in her.

The bell of the church began to chime. She followed a group of local women inside, and sat by herself in the rear. She felt an urge to pray, and was afraid to do so. In the semi-darkness she watched the people drift in.

A young girl in a pink dress came in to the confessional and knelt. Irene could just hear the gentle sound of her voice and that of the priest answering her. In a short time the girl left. She looked radiantly happy, and Irene's eyes filled with tears. How little the child could have had to confess, what trivial sins! She would have liked to go to the confessional and pour out her entire story. It would bring no gentle smile to the listener's lips, as the confession of that young girl must have done. With what horror would he hear her?

She and that priest were of different kingdoms, she knew that now: his was the realm of light, and hers of darkness.

A group of young men from the seminary beyond the village filed in. Some of them were quite young, and she wondered what they could know already of sin and horror. Had any of them known agony such as hers? Had their faith been so tested, would they be able now to pray? She saw no anguish on their faces, and she resented their aura of peace and happiness.

The canons of the church followed, and finally, the officiating priest. She sat through the entire ceremony, and though she thought it beautiful, it did not move her. She felt a growing weight in her heart.

'God has abandoned me,' she said to herself with conviction. She was alone in a foreign land, she was surrounded by evil, and here in the temple of God she could find no solace. Even here, she had only to close her eyes to see the mocking face of M. Gastion.

She began to cry, and because she knew that there was no hope for her, she got up and left the church, and went back to the house. She did not encounter Elliot, and she did not know if he even realized she had been away. She wondered what he would say if she told him, and why. He would not believe her. He would think she was homesick.

M. Gastion was still in his room. He greeted her with a knowing smile and a

133

nod, as if he knew every conflicting thought that had gone through her mind since she had left him.

'I'll do as you ask,' she said, coming to kneel on the floor beside him. 'I'll write my sister and ask her to come for a visit.'

He looked pleased. 'It will be for the best, you shall see,' he said.

That she could not believe. She knew that what she was doing was evil and would bring ruin down upon Emily's innocent head. She could not help herself.

'I'm so unhappy,' she cried.

'Don't be.' He put a hand on her head and gently stroked her hair. 'I command you to be happy.'

A weight was lifted from her then, and whatever bitter struggle had been going on within her was ended. She suddenly thought how easy it would be to deceive Emily, just as she had deceived Elliot, and she felt elated with a sense of power.

She gave a little laugh and, turning her face, kissed his hand.

PART 2

EMILY

14

Oh! yet a little while
May I behold in thee what I was once,
My dear, dear Sister!
—William Wordsworth

Los Angeles was having one of those inexplicable hot spells that sometimes hit in the early spring. The weather was sticky, the air-conditioning seemed unable to cope with both heat and humidity.

Emily had just come from her bath and already she felt soiled with perspiration. She was annoyed with herself because she had so tied herself up with appointments and meetings that she had to stay in L.A. at the present and could not get away.

Why she had managed things in that fashion she had no idea. If she had any sense at all, she would have been on the Spanish coast right this moment. No, the best place to be just now was Maine. That would be ideal, and Maine was not beyond the realm of possibility, if she could juggle a few appointments.

She thought of southern France and of Irene. It would be nice there just now. Irene was off the beaten track, and anyway, southern France did not get really buffeted by the tourist hordes until summer.

The thought of Irene made her ask herself, not for the first time, what exactly was going on with her sister. She unfolded the letter that had just come from Irene and read it again.

A great deal of the letter was about some man they had met who, as nearly as Emily could make out, was living with them while they restored the house. Now, in New York or Los Angeles, that would mean just one thing. For that matter, it generally meant the same thing in France, maybe even more than elsewhere, but not with Irene and Elliot. She knew them too well to suspect that.

Yet, there was something about the way Irene described this M. Gastion: ' . . . the most unbearably sensual man I've ever seen. It's impossible to look at him without wanting to be locked in his arms, kissing him. His mouth, his eyes, his body . . . '

There was more, that went into such detail as to be shocking, doubly so because it came from Irene, and Emily had never known her to write or talk in this manner. In fact, if she did not recognize the handwriting and the signature as being unquestionably Irene's, she would have thought surely there had been some mistake and the letter had been written by someone else.

She shook her head. There was hardly any doubt. The words with which Irene wrote of M. Gastion were the words of love, and not of the spiritual sort, either.

Nor was that the end of the mystery. In the time the couple had been in France, Irene had written her again and again of her unhappiness with the place, of her fears and her annoyance at how slowly the restoration was progressing. She had hardly had anything nice to say on the subject, but now, out of the blue, were words of bountiful praise.

' . . . I can't think how I ever found the

place dreary. It's most extraordinarily beautiful. Truthfully, I feel as if I have always lived here, not just all my life, but forever, and that I will continue forever after.'

Emily heard Mrs. Osgood come in the back way. The housekeeper 'made noises' in the kitchen for a moment or so, her way of being discreet, before she came into the living room.

'Good Heavens,' she said, coming to stand in the doorway and look at Emily, 'you look as if the Internal Revenue just refused to accept your figures.'

Emily gave her a distracted smile. 'No, I got a letter from Irene.'

'Well, no one would refuse to accept her figure. There isn't anything wrong with her, is there?' Mrs. Osgood had served as Emily's housekeeper for several years, and she was fond of her mistress and of her sister as well. She regarded Irene as 'a bit of fluff,' but sweet and gentle, 'the kind that wants looking after,' as she had often put it.

'I wish I knew,' Emily said. She sighed. 'I suppose I had better do as she suggests and go for a visit. It sounds as if things are going a little astray.'

Mrs. Osgood, who had a knack for reading between the lines, said, 'If Irene is unhappy, wouldn't it make more sense to bring her here?'

'You know, sometimes I don't think you're such an old fool after all,' Emily said with a smile.

Her housekeeper grunted and went back to her kitchen. Emily thought for a moment longer, then went to the telephone and dialed the number of an old friend.

'Marcia, Emily Hastings,' she said into the phone. 'Darling, are you using your place at Big Sur for a few weeks? Great, would you mind . . . ? You've no idea how much I appreciate it. Look, let's have drinks sometime soon.'

Afterward, she wrote two letters, one to Irene and one to Elliot. In the first, she pleaded engagements for several weeks, but begged Irene to come here for a visit. In the second, she was more frank.

★　★　★

'I still say this is utterly silly,' Irene said, 'I can't think why all of a sudden you want to throw money around like this.' She caught a curious glance from a passing woman and gave her a frosty look in return. She did not really care if everyone in the air terminal heard her. She was furious with Elliot for practically forcing her to take this trip. He had not even asked in advance. He had simply shown up one evening with the ticket, and told her he was sending her home for a visit with Emily.

'It isn't throwing money around. In the first place, you need to get away. You're looking peaked, and you know nothing in the world is more important to me than your health. In the second place, it's about time we had our things shipped and you can arrange that while you're there.'

'That's the silliest thing of all. The moving company has all our things in storage, ready to ship them when we give the word. All we have to do is write and tell them when and where. Anyway, they are in New York, and I will be in L.A.'

'I don't trust moving people.' They were announcing her flight. A line had queued up already, tickets in hand. 'Anyway, you've been dying of homesickness since we arrived here. You must have told me a thousand times that you wanted to go back to the U.S.'

'But that was before.'

'Before what?'

'Before — before I got used to the place. Elliot, I don't want to leave, truly I don't.'

They had reached the checkpoint and the uniformed man was holding his hand out for Irene's ticket. Elliot took it from her and handed it to him.

'It's all settled, sweetheart.' He bent forward to kiss her. 'What on earth's that?'

She was wearing a little wrought silver ball on a chain. It was hollow and contained something. He could not see what it was, but coming so close, he could certainly smell it, and it was not pleasant.

'It's a charm. For good luck while traveling.'

'I've never seen it before.'

'Philippe gave it to me.'

He had never before heard her refer to M. Gastion by his given name, and was about to comment on it, but they announced her last call just then. The man at the gate fidgeted anxiously. Elliot kissed her and shoved her through before she could object again. He watched her walk away, not hurrying, but reluctantly. He could not imagine why she suddenly didn't want to go. She'd wanted to return badly enough before. He paused in mid-thought, and asked himself the same question he had asked her a moment earlier: before what?

He had another reason for being happy to send his wife back to America for a visit. Just a few days before, Gastion had brought up the subject of Elliot's writing.

'I'm afraid I've rather neglected it since we came here,' Elliot had admitted ruefully. 'But I hope to get back to it before long.'

'There is no time like the present,' M. Gastion said. 'Your wife will be away for a few days. This would be an excellent time for you to begin. That way I can look over your shoulder and perhaps I can be of some help to you. I know a thing or two about writing, you know, and I have friends in publishing circles. I would not be surprised if we could get your next work published.'

'I don't even know what to start on.'

'I have an idea.' M. Gastion outlined briefly the idea he had in mind. Elliot listened attentively. As he listened, he grew increasingly excited. This could be the opportunity he had been waiting for. He didn't care what the book was about, if Gastion wanted it, and could get it published. He would write on anything. It was only a bonus that Gastion's idea actually sounded promising.

'Of course, I should be working on the house.'

Gastion quickly made light of that. 'Leave that to me. No, really, I mean it. It is almost done anyway. You bring your typewriter out here, on the terrace. The view will help inspire you.'

So, when he left the airport after seeing Irene off, Elliot was not only relieved and confident that he had solved the problem of her seeming distraction, but he looked eagerly forward to returning to the house and to work on his new book.

He could not explain why, but he felt instinctively that Gastion would help him immensely.

15

The stars move still, time runs,
the clock will strike,
The devil will come, and
Faustus must be damn'd.
O, I'll leap up to my God:
who pulls me down?
See, see where Christ's blood
streams in the firmament.
One drop would save my soul,
half a drop . . .
—Christopher Marlowe

Emily was shocked to see how much Irene had changed.

Yet it was difficult to pinpoint just what and where the changes were. She expected to find Irene tired after the flight, and after her letters, she expected her to be unhappy.

In fact, though, Irene looked only a little rumpled from the trip. What she had was an air of dissolution, as if she had been living a particularly sensuous and restless life. The gentle, soft-voiced creature of the past seemed to have been replaced by another woman, coarse and shrill. Irene had always dressed in exquisite taste. Now her look was flamboyant and even vulgar. The colors of her costume were all wrong, and she had painted on her makeup with a cheap effect, like an entertainer in a tawdry nightclub.

Emily tried to tell herself that Irene had been under a strain, and that this change in her was only proof of the wisdom of her suggestion, that Irene come for a rest.

Irene was even a little subdued in greeting her. They embraced and laughed and kissed one another, but Emily had the odd impression Irene was only going through the motions.

It took some time to finish with customs and get the baggage to the car. Finally, however, they were on their way.

'I have a surprise for you,' Emily said as they pulled out of the parking lot. 'We're not going to stay in Los Angeles at all. We're going to Big Sur.'

She expected this news to be welcome.

They had shared a vacation trip to Big Sur years before and had always talked of it afterwards as one of their nicest times together.

To her surprise, however, Irene was disappointed.

* * *

'I still don't understand it,' Irene was saying for perhaps the fourth time as they arrived at the cottage on the rugged California coast. 'You were too busy to come to France, but as soon as I arrive, you whisk me away up here to Big Sur, a full day's drive from Los Angeles.'

Emily was making an effort to be especially sweet tempered, although her nerves were rapidly becoming frayed. Irene was not just being difficult, she was downright shrewish.

'I told you,' she said, setting her bags in the middle of the floor. 'I was able to wriggle out of some engagements and the others I conveniently forgot. I've been begging Marcia for years to let me borrow this place, and when she called and said it was free and would I like to use it, it just seemed the most perfect idea. I thought you'd love it. And I can't think why you're complaining so. Frankly, you look as if you could do with a rest. It's none of my business, I know, but tell me, dear, has Elliot been working you around the clock, or what?'

She meant this to be a joke, to relieve some of the tension between them, but Irene failed to see any humor in it.

'I think I ought to have been told sooner,' Irene said petulantly. She looked around the cottage, which Emily thought charming, and wrinkled her nose a little.

'Of, course, it is rustic,' Emily said lightly.

Irene went to the window and pulled the drapes. It was just sunset, and the view was dramatic, a sweeping vista of rocks, and the darkening ocean.

It reminded Irene of the landscapes she had seen in her dreams with Philippe Gastion. The rocks looked sharp and threatening, the waves were black. Even the clouds that hung low in the sky were eerie.

She said, in a sharp voice, 'I'm sorry I'm here. I didn't want to come. Elliot made me. I only mean to stay for a day or two.'

Emily was shocked by Irene's violent tone. She looked at her sister and was frightened to see not a trace of affection.

'Of course, dear, if you'd rather not stay. You know I want nothing more than your happiness.'

Suddenly Irene burst into tears. Emily put her arms about her. She was mystified by this display of changing emotions, but moved by Irene's evident unhappiness.

'There, there,' she murmured. 'It's all right. You've been unhappy and you've had a long trip, and you're feeling out of sorts. Come on, let me put you to bed, and you'll feel one hundred percent better after a nap.'

Irene mumbled something through her tears, but Emily paid no attention. She steered her sister gently but firmly toward the bedroom.

'Now, you lie here, and I absolutely forbid you to get up without my permission. I'm going to fix you some nice hot chocolate.'

Emily hurried out to the kitchen. She found everything she needed, and in matter of a few minutes had two steaming mugs of chocolate on a tray.

She did not take them directly to the bedroom. It was evident to her that Irene was highly overwrought, and that what she needed most just now was a long night's sleep.

She found her sleeping pills and crushed two of them and stirred the powder into Irene's chocolate. That was enough to guarantee a horse a good night's sleep, she thought with a grim smile. She carried the tray into the bedroom.

Irene was where she had left her, lying across the bed. She had stopped crying, though, and looked altogether calm. She smiled when Emily came in.

'Feeling better?' Emily asked.

'Much, thank you. I'm afraid I've been awful. Forgive me, please.'

'You know I do,' Emily said, kissing her cheek.

'But,' Irene sipped the chocolate, 'I do

want to get back to France as soon as possible, and I want you to come with me. You must promise you will, please.' She smiled in her most coaxing fashion. It was the same look and the same tone of voice that she had used when they were children, and had set herself to persuading Emily of something. And yet, something about her manner was disquieting.

'Yes, of course, if it's so important to you. No, drink the rest of that.'

'It is important.' Irene smiled with what might have been a look of triumph.

Deliberately, Emily changed the subject. She talked of mutual friends in New York, and of a new apartment she was considering, and of a hundred different subjects, all firmly unrelated to France. Finally, after what seemed to her far too long a time, Irene's head began to nod, and her eyelids to droop. Soon afterward she was sound asleep.

Emily bent over her and removed Irene's shoes and her wristwatch. She saw Irene was wearing a little silver ornament on a chain, and that it had become tightly twisted about her throat. Afraid that the chain might break, she undid it and slipped it off Irene's throat.

At that precise moment, Irene gave a low cry.

It must only have been some passing dream, however, because once the pendant was gone, Irene gave a deep sigh and sank deeper into the pillow. Her face relaxed and she looked profoundly untroubled.

Curious, Emily examined the pendant. It was not unattractive, and appeared to be quite old, but it had a peculiar odor that was unpleasant, to say the least. She put the ornament on the dresser, but when she came into the room a little later to see if Irene was still asleep, the entire room was permeated with the odd smell.

She put it instead in a box, and put that in the spare bedroom.

16

This is the night
That either makes me or
fordoes me quite.
—William Shakespeare

Emily lay in a trance, awake and yet completely unthinking. Her mind hung suspended somewhere in the universe, apart from herself. A gull came laughing down from the sky, into her range of vision. It challenged a wave and then disappeared upward again. The ocean roared its approval.

'Emily.' She lifted her head and looked around.

'Here, look.'

Irene had just emerged from the water, scrambling onto the rocks below. She waved and lifted a huge starfish for Emily to see.

Emily nodded her approval, not sure whether the gesture would carry so far.

She glanced at her watch. 'It's nearly lunchtime.'

Irene nodded and put the starfish with her other acquisitions in a sheltered tidal basin where, sooner or later, the tide would carry them all right back to sea.

'Then I'll simply collect them again,' Irene had said when Emily made that observation. She began to clamber over the rocks to join her sister.

Watching her approach, Emily was struck by her sister's youthful vivacity. Irene did indeed look like a schoolgirl, carefree and gloriously happy, in sharp contrast to the week before. The transformation had been truly incredible.

'If this salt air does as much for me,' Emily had said the night before, 'I shall never have to use a facial mask again.'

She lay back upon her piece of rock and closed her eyes, and let the sun caress her bare arms and legs. It was a long climb from the water to where she was sunbathing, and there was no particular need to hurry.

She was almost asleep when Irene, standing over her, squeezed some of the water from her bathing suit. The cold water brought Emily awake with a start. Irene laughed mischievously.

'Now I know how I can wake you in the mornings, you slugabed,' she said. 'I'll throw you back in that water and hold you under.' Emily took a slap at Irene's foot. Irene grabbed a towel and began to dry herself. 'Here, get my back.'

'I ought to take sticks to it,' Emily grumbled, but she got up and began to dry her sister's back with the towel. To her surprise, Irene turned and gave her an impetuous hug. 'Oh, Emily, I'm so deliciously happy here.'

Emily nodded and began to collect their things. 'A week ago, you could think of nothing but going back to France.'

'I never want to go back there.' Her tone was so vehement that Emily bit her lip, thinking she had strayed into dangerous territory again.

'I mean it,' Irene said when they were on the path back to the house. 'I hate it there. It's loathsome. And he's there.'

'Elliot?' Emily was astonished.

'No, M. Gastion.'

'Oh.' That man whom Irene had described in such sensuous terms in her letter. She would have liked to know more about him, but she was frankly afraid to pursue the subject.

'He's horrible.' Irene dropped her voice almost to a whisper, as if someone might overhear. 'I can't begin to tell you — there are things . . . '

Emily felt the time was not yet right for such intimate confessions. She wanted Irene back in the happier mood of a few moments before, and, if she were completely honest with herself, she was a bit afraid of what she might hear.

'There's no need to explain anything to me. And as for going back, if you're really that unhappy about it, I'll write to Elliot personally, and tell him that you've simply got to stay for an extended visit.'

They entered the kitchen. They didn't bother to lock the house, because no one ever came by this isolated point.

'Poor Elliot. I haven't even written to tell him I'm here. He thinks I'm in Los Angeles.'

'Don't trouble your pretty head about

that. I wrote to him right after we got here, to tell him where we'd be. I didn't want him thinking I had kidnapped you.'

Emily went through into the bedroom but Irene paused in the kitchen and frowned. 'Then he knows. He knows where I am.'

'Elliot? Of course, I just said I wrote to him.'

'When I first came,' Irene said, hesitating in the bedroom doorway, 'the first day — you said something about a pendant I was wearing.'

'I took it off you, yes, while you were sleeping. I told you, it smelled awful. I put it in the extra bedroom. Isn't it there?'

'I haven't gone to look. I — would you, please?'

'Of course. Do you want it now?'

Irene nodded. Emily slipped into a robe. She found the charm just where she had left it. The odor had grown even worse.

'What's in this thing, anyway? It smells like a dead animal.'

'I don't know.'

Emily held the pendant out to her, but

159

Irene did not take it. She stared at it in a strange way. It was almost, Emily thought, as if she were afraid of it, and yet she seemed at the same time fascinated. The expression on Irene's face sent a shiver along her spine.

'Look, I really think something has spoiled in this. Why don't I put it outside until I can clean it?'

Irene looked as if she had been released from a spell. Her shoulders drooped and her eyelids fluttered. 'No, I want you to take it outside and throw it as far into the ocean as you can.'

'Well, I know it smells bad but I do think it can be cleaned up and deodorized, so to speak. It's actually an attractive piece and I think it's valuable.'

'Not to me. Throw it away, please.'

Emily shrugged. 'If you like. Do you mean now?'

'Now. Right away.'

Emily took the pendant and went outside, to the bluff overhanging the ocean and the rocky beach below. She looked at the silver ornament on its chain, and hesitated.

It really was a lovely piece, and it was foolish to toss it into the ocean simply because it smelled bad from something spoiled inside it. Indeed, she thought the smell had diminished already. If she could get it opened — or, maybe she wouldn't even have to do that. If it were soaked in a good disinfectant for a day or so, and then cleaned in water, Irene would no doubt be pleasantly surprised to have it back, wearable once again.

She made a pretense of throwing the charm into the ocean and dropped it instead into her pocket.

Inside, she found that Irene had fallen asleep across the bed. Although it had been no more than a few minutes, she was in a deep sleep already. While Emily stood in the doorway, Irene moaned softly and turned her head to and fro, as if she were having a bad dream.

Emily went to the kitchen and put the ornament on a high shelf over the kitchen window. It really didn't smell as badly as it had before, which only served to confirm her opinion that it was, after all, redeemable. Later, she would clean it. For now, she wanted a shower.

She went into the bathroom, and in a moment had forgotten all about the silver pendant.

17

The other shape,
If shape it might be call'd
that shape had none
Distinguishable in member,
joint, or limb,
Or substance might be call'd
that shadow seem'd,
For each seem'd either.
—John Milton

Irene was still asleep when Emily came out of the bathroom. She had tossed and turned so much that the bedcovers were all twisted around her.

Emily watched her from the foot of the bed. Irene appeared to be dreaming of some sort of struggle, as if she were engaged in mortal combat. Her face was contorted with anguish. She moaned faintly and lifted her hands to ward off some enemy.

Thinking it might be best to wake her, Emily bent down to touch Irene's face. At once she brought her hand back with a jerk. Irene's skin was hot to the touch. She was burning up with a fever.

It was incredible. Only a short time before, Irene had seemed in the best of health. When they came back from swimming, Irene had looked and acted as if she felt fine, and there had been no sign of a fever only a short time before. It had come up all of a sudden — in a span of fifteen or twenty minutes, she felt as if she were on fire.

It scarcely seemed possible.

★   ★   ★

The fever lasted for three days. The local doctor came and told Emily there was a virus going around and prescribed the usual aspirins, fluids and rest.

Emily left Irene's side as little as possible. Regularly, she roused her sister enough to give her aspirin and liquids — fruit juices, mostly, and warm soup. Between times, she bathed her again and again with cold cloths, trying to keep the fever down.

Throughout the siege, Irene's tortured dreams continued. Sometimes Emily caught feverish words and phrases. 'No,' she cried often, and several times she begged someone to 'Let me free.' She would thrash about, turning her head from side to side, and sometimes lash out with her hands, like a bird beating with her wings at the cage that held her.

On the third night, weak with exhaustion, Emily dreamed too. She fell asleep in a big chair she had pulled up to the bedside. Irene's condition was unchanged from what it had been when the fever began. Her skin was burning to the touch, and she thrashed about restlessly.

Emily thought she had no more than closed her eyes when she heard a sound and, opening them, she saw a man in the room. She moved as if to sit up and demand of him who he was, but she found that she could neither move nor speak.

He was dressed in black and silver, in an outfit that looked antiquated. She thought him singularly unattractive, with a pale, wasted look. His mouth was sensuous and cruel, and his eyes, when he chanced to look in her direction, had a hard, almost inhuman glint.

He had no more than a glance for her. It was Irene who interested him. He went to the bed and reached down to take her hand in his. To Emily's amazement, Irene opened her eyes at once and sat up.

The visitor kissed Irene. This was no kiss of simple affection, either, but one of gross passion. Again Emily tried to move, to object, but she could do neither.

The two at the bed were talking, in voices so low that Emily could hear only a murmur. Irene's hand went to her throat and, puzzled, she glanced in Emily's direction and whispered something. He too looked her way briefly. His eyes met Emily's and she shuddered.

To her horror, he rose from the bed and came slowly toward her with an insinuating smile. He bent over her, and she wanted to shrink away from him, to disappear into the depths of the chair.

He put his mouth to her ear. She heard his voice, low and coaxing, and felt his hand gently stroke her temple, but she could not tell what it was he said.

She woke with a start, her heart pounding. She was drenched with sweat. For a moment she did not remember; then the image of the man in her dream flashed before her eyes. She leapt from her chair and looked wildly about the room. So real had her dream been that she fully expected to see the man in black standing nearby, but the room was empty. Irene was asleep as before. Everything was as it had been. It had only been a dream after all.

Her throat was dry and parched. She went into the kitchen. She had just gotten herself a glass of water from the tap when she heard a sound at the door.

In New York or Los Angeles, she might have been frightened. She did not know the time, but it was certainly the middle of the night. Strangely, she did not now feel any fear. She was hardly even surprised at the sound. She had an odd sense of expectancy.

Her visitor was nothing more frightening than a large black cat, who had decided that hers was a likely door at which to beg.

It had begun to rain. She was much too softhearted to make him stay out in the weather.

'Do all cats have an instinct for knowing where to find a pushover,' she asked, letting him in.

He purred loudly and rubbed against her bare leg. He was certainly an affectionate beast. She was reminded of that cat in Paris. She seemed to have an attraction for large black cats. For a moment, she had an impulse to check his paws, to see if he had the same scar.

'Don't be a goose,' she told herself. To the cat, she said, 'I suppose all this affection is leading up to a bowl of milk? Well, come on, I'll heat some for both of us.'

She heated a saucepan of milk and poured herself a cup, and put the rest into a bowl for her visitor, who took to it enthusiastically.

She sat and sipped her milk thoughtfully, recalling the dream she'd had, but the details were already fading, and she could not think why she had been so shaken by it.

She finished her milk and realized that while she had been sitting and thinking, the cat had finished his and had disappeared somewhere. She rinsed out the cup and the bowl and left them in the sink, and went in search of him.

'So here you are.' He was on the bed with Irene, curled up against her as if he had settled down for the night.

'I think,' she said, 'that might be a mistake. Why don't you share the chair with me, if you feel you must have company.'

She picked him up and put him in her chair. He did not seem to object to the change. He looked up at her with an understanding expression, and continued to purr loudly.

She put a hand to Irene's forehead. Her fever had gone down a little, and she was sleeping better. Perhaps the danger was past.

She joined the cat in the chair. He wriggled about until he was lying upon her breast. She could feel as well as hear his purring, and she could feel ever so faintly his breath upon her throat. Far from discomforting her, however, his presence had a soothing quality.

'If I could find some way to patent it,' she murmured, stroking his soft hair, 'I think it would make a wonderful tranquilizing device.'

She had no difficulty at all in falling asleep again, and if she dreamed this time, she did not recall it afterward.

18

I dreamed, and dream it still.
—G. K. Chesterton

By morning Irene was recovered. She was still weak, and Emily thought that she would surely have to look forward to a few days yet of resting in bed until she could get her strength back, but for the first time in three days she was truly conscious, and aware of her surroundings.

In fact, when Emily awoke, Irene was sitting up in bed, regarding her in — it seemed to Emily — a peculiar fashion. For a few seconds Emily looked back at her sleepily. The significance occurred to her then and she sat up abruptly.

'Good morning,' she said. 'You're awake and sitting up. How do you feel?' She jumped up and came to the bed, feeling for the fever. It was gone.

'I feel fine,' Irene said. 'Completely fine,' but her voice was flat and dull, but one could not expect all traces of her illness to vanish with a snap of the fingers.

'Thank God.' Her eyes fell just then on the silver ornament lying across her sister's breast. 'Why, when on earth did you get that back? I had it hidden away until I could clean it up for you. I was going to surprise you.'

'You put it around my neck during the night.'

'I? I did not such thing.'

'But of course you did. I woke at some point. The fever had broken, apparently, and for the first time I was aware of things again. It was only for a moment, but I clearly remember you bending over me and fastening the chain around my throat.'

'And I as clearly remember doing no such thing. You must have been dreaming, and got up yourself, and put it on. Only . . . ' She paused and frowned. 'How did you know where it was, or that I hadn't really thrown it away before?'

'Exactly.'

'Oh, I know, the odor.'

'The odor has gone.'

It was true, but Emily still could not

credit the suggestion that she had gotten up during the night and put the pendant around Irene's neck. She rather vaguely felt that Irene must have gotten up herself, and somehow found it. As feverish as she had been, it was entirely possible she might do so and afterward not only not remember doing it, but think she remembered another scene altogether.

This little puzzlement, however, was nothing compared to what was in store for her. The very next thing Irene said was, 'I want to go back to France.'

Emily stared at her in amazement. 'But, just a few days ago, you never wanted to go back.'

'Oh, that was the virus talking. I was feeling rotten, and cross about everything, but I'm better now, and I want to go back, at once, and I want you to come with me. I won't take no for an answer.'

Emily's head was whirling. She sat on the edge of the bed and took Irene's hand in hers. 'Darling, you know I will do anything I can to make you happy. If you truly want to go back to France, we assuredly shall, but you need to rest first, and get your strength back.'

'Nonsense, you know I'm basically as strong as a horse. I'll be out of bed today, and by tomorrow we can leave here.' She cast a glance around the room and twisted her face in an ugly grimace. 'I hate this place.'

'I think that may be rushing it a little. You've been quite sick, really. I think you should wait at least a few days before you even try to get out of bed, and then . . . '

Irene slapped her hand away. 'I won't be kept here like a prisoner,' she said sharply. 'I'm leaving tomorrow, I don't care what you say.'

For a moment, Emily had an urge to take hold of her sister's shoulders and shake her fiercely. She restrained herself. Irene had indeed been sick, and she was just not entirely rational at the moment. It would be pointless, even cruel, to argue with her just now.

'If you really feel that strongly,' she said in an even tone of voice, 'we'll drive back to Los Angeles tomorrow, to my apartment, and you can leave for France whenever you wish, of course. I didn't mean to seem as if I were making a prisoner of you.'

Again Irene's mood changed in an instant. She smiled in a coaxing way and found Emily's hand again, squeezing it.

'And you will come with me, won't you, please?'

'Well, I can't leave at the snap of a finger. If I'm going to France, there are things I'll need to arrange.'

'I'll help you with everything. We'll be ready to go in no time.'

Emily tried to respond to Irene's smiling enthusiasm, but she felt depressed rather than cheered by it. 'I can't see why it's so vital that I go with you. I could just as easily come later.'

'I want you with me. You're my sister, and I love you.'

This last statement, however, was said in such a flat and unemotional way that it fell falsely on the ear. The entire scene, in fact, made Emily somewhat uncomfortable, something that had never occurred before between them.

'Whatever you like. I'm going to make some coffee. Do you think you'd like to have a cup this morning, if you're feeling so much better?'

'I'd love one — and, Emily, are there any cigarettes in the house?'

'Why, yes, I think I saw a pack in one of the kitchen cabinets. Why?'

Irene smiled innocently, and plumped up the pillow behind her back. 'I would like one, of course,' she said.

'Of course? But I've never seen you smoke a cigarette before.'

'Well, if you like, you may sit and watch me smoke one now. If, that is, you will bring me one.' She cocked a mischievous eyebrow.

'Of course,' Emily said, a little dazed, and went to the kitchen to find the cigarettes. It was not until she had brought the cigarette back, and watched Irene actually light it and begin to puff on it, that she remembered the black cat she had let into the house during the night.

'Oh, the cat,' she said, looking around.

'What cat?'

'A big black one. It scratched at the kitchen door last night and I let it in. It came in here and curled up in the chair with me. I wonder where it's gotten to?'

'I didn't see any black cat. Are you sure you didn't dream it?'

'No, I — there was a cat.' Emily gave her head a shake. The events of the night were so muddled. That business with the silver pendant and now the cat that ought to be here, but evidently wasn't. She *had* been very tired herself . . . was she confusing dream with reality? She remembered something, something about a dream — but the thought was too slippery, it eluded her grasp and faded like the smoke from Irene's cigarette.

Irene was smiling as if she knew a secret. 'If there was one, where is he now?'

'I don't know.' Emily went through the house, but she found no trace of the cat, nor any obvious means by which he might have left without her opening a door for him.

That was only the half of it, too. She found no evidence either that he had ever been there. She remembered giving him milk in a bowl, but there was no dirty bowl in the kitchen. She found the saucepan in which she had heated the milk, and the oversized mug from which she'd had hers, but there was no bowl, neither dirty, nor rinsed and put on the counter with the other two items.

It was so real in her mind, that she could hardly believe the cat's visit was a dream. She could see him clearly in her mind's eye. More than that, she could hear him, that loud purring of his, and feel him rub against her.

Or had he? If it had not been a dream, then where was the cat, and where was the bowl in which she had given him the milk? She looked in the cupboard, and counted the bowls that were there. If one took it for granted that the bowls, like the dishes and the cups, numbered eight, then all of the bowls to the set were in the cupboard. She could hardly suppose the cat had washed its own bowl and put it away, before letting himself out of the house.

Irene teased her about it later, amused by her sister's confusion. 'You're just being stubborn. You know it was only a dream. You got all confused in your sleep, and you don't even remember putting the pendant around my neck.'

Try though she might, Emily could not recall doing anything of the sort. 'There must be some logical explanation for everything,' she insisted, but a bit lamely.

'Of course there is. It's quite simple, really. You brought a cat into the house and gave it some milk, and the cat found the pendant and hung it about my neck, and then he washed up his bowl and put it away in the cupboard, and let himself out again.' She gave a coarse laugh that grated unpleasantly on Emily's nerves.

19

Thy heart with dead, wing'd
Innocencies fill'd,
Ev'n as a nest with birds
After the old ones by the hawk are kill'd.
—Coventry Patmore

'What a good-looking doorman,' Irene said when the elevator doors had closed upon them. 'Haven't you tried to lure him up to your apartment yet?'

They had driven down that afternoon from Big Sur. It had been an unpleasant drive, to Emily's way of thinking.

'To tell the truth, I hadn't even noticed the man before. Is he good-looking?' It was not entirely true — she had noticed the man before, and he was good-looking, but she was offended by the suggestion that she might try to 'lure him' up to her apartment for some reason.

She was barely able to keep her voice even. She was in a bad temper. Irene's company, which she had always enjoyed in the past, was grating badly on her nerves.

'You hadn't noticed?' Irene gave an incredulous little laugh. 'Darling, you are peculiar, I must say, not to notice him. I'm sure he would make a wonderful lover. Have you a lover, by the way? I don't believe you've said.'

Emily very nearly said, 'That is none of your business.' The words were on the tip of her tongue, but she checked herself. 'The way you talk. Honestly, I can't think what's gotten into you.'

Irene only laughed again, a laugh Emily had quickly and especially come to dislike.

The elevator doors opened. Emily was grateful for any diversion that spared her the necessity of continuing these vulgar dialogues. If she had not known otherwise, she would almost have believed that this woman was not Irene at all, but an impostor. No one could be less like Irene in her behavior or her conversation or her attitudes, but there was no denying that it was Irene, at least physically. It was almost, Emily had concluded in a moment of fancy, as if someone else had taken over Irene's physical body, someone who was coarse and vulgar and licentious.

The apartment was quiet. 'It's Mrs. Osgood's day off,' Emily said. 'We'll have to rough it, I'm afraid. Why don't you get comfortable and I'll fix us some coffee.'

'Make it a drink for me,' Irene said. She threw her coat over a chair and made her way to the bathroom, ignoring the guest room off the hall and going instead toward the one in Emily's bedroom.

She was surprised to see a large, glossy photograph of Elliot taped to the mirror of Emily's dresser. She recognized the picture, one that had been taken a few years ago. It was a flattering likeness — she herself had always thought it was the best one ever taken of him.

The sight of it like this, in Emily's bedroom, jarred. It was like the pictures that young girls taped up of their favorite beaus, or movie star idols, and in a flash, Irene saw the photograph's significance. She realized suddenly what she had never noticed before, although it had been right under her nose: Emily was in love with Elliot.

It was so astounding that for a second or two it seemed absurd, but the doubts faded almost at once.

If she had needed any confirmation of the fact, she got it in the quick look of alarm that crossed Emily's face when she came into the room and realized that she had forgotten to take the picture down from what was plainly its accustomed place.

'I was surprised to see Elliot up there,' Irene said in a sly manner. 'Don't you feel odd, having him watch you sleep, so to speak?'

Emily recovered her poise quickly. 'I had it up to study the bone structure,' she said, carrying their jackets to the closet to hang them up. 'I was taking that drawing class at the university, you remember, I wrote you about it, and Elliot made an excellent model, at least in his photographs. He has a really fine bone structure.'

'I always said so.'

Later, when Emily had gone out for

some shopping, Irene went back to the bedroom. The photograph had been taken down, but she found it in a drawer, along with literally dozens of others. Emily appeared to have every picture that had ever been taken of Elliot, nor did the fact that others were also in many of them fool her for a moment. It was blatantly obvious that it was Elliot whose photos Emily had been collecting.

She told herself that Emily was no less deceitful than she. She was suddenly furious that Emily dared love her husband, and she even allowed herself to wonder briefly if anything had ever occurred between the two of them, but she immediately dismissed that idea. Elliot was such a fool, the truth would have been written all over him. He hadn't the cleverness to engage in an affair, without letting it be known. Emily might have been able to pull it off, and probably would have been glad to, but Elliot was too much a fool.

Her anger passed and she decided the situation was very amusing. She thought of all the times the three of them had been together. What a torture it must have been for her sister. She recalled how Emily had met Elliot first and, having obviously fallen in love with him at once, had brought him to the apartment, only to have him fall hopelessly in love with her instead. It must have been a great humiliation.

Irene went to the mirror and studied her reflection in it. Why had she never before realized the extent of her beauty, or the power that it gave her over others? With all her intelligence and poise, Emily was weak in contrast to her.

It had taken Philippe Gastion to give her an awareness of what was within her, hidden even from her own sight until he had revealed it.

'Philippe,' she breathed his name. She seemed almost to see his reflection beside her own in the glass. She fingered the wrought silver ornament at her breast and a shudder of sensuous desire went through her body.

★ ★ ★

M. Bernard and the local doctor, M. Florimond, were having a glass of wine at the little sidewalk café in the village, when someone sat down at the table with them. They glanced up, and into the round, pink face of the abbé.

'*Mon ami*,' M. Bernard said, gesturing, 'Will you have some wine?'

'Perhaps it would help to digest my lunch,' the abbé said. 'I confess, the cabbage the sisters prepared seems to have grown heavier since I ate it.'

Another glass was called for and brought, and when the abbé had taken a sip of it, he said, 'I was up at the château yesterday for a visit.'

M. Bernard made a gesture of disgust. 'Faugh, they fired me, so that the jackanapes could take over.' But after a moment he gave a shrug and said, 'To tell you the truth, I was glad to be done with it.'

'You did not like the American couple?' the Doctor asked.

'Very much, in fact. They are foolish innocents, like all Americans. They know nothing about life, and they think they know everything, but they were nice, and she was such a sweet creature.'

His faced darkened again. 'It saddens me, to think of them there.' He looked up and into the abbé's eyes. 'Mark my words, there's evil there. The sort of evil that they would scoff at, with all their electricity and modern toilets, but the kind of evil we three understand, eh?'

The abbé took another nervous sip of his wine. He had had thoughts that were not dissimilar, and had tried to keep them from his mind, but they kept troubling him, and they had led him to pay a call on the young husband yesterday. He had not liked what he saw.

'The wife is away, you know,' he said.

'So I heard,' the Doctor said.

'And the husband?' Bernard asked. 'How is he? Still under the thumb of that Gastion?'

'Gastion was away himself for a few days, it seems, although he is back today. And M. Lewis is writing a new book.'

M. Bernard nodded his head. 'I suppose that is good.'

"I am not so certain. There was

something — I do not quite know what — something about the way he was writing, about his attitude. I cannot seem to put it into words, but it was as if he were driven. He looked as if he had not eaten for a day or so, and he plainly had not taken time to shave or bathe. And all the while I was there, I could not help but see he was eager for me to go so that he could return to his work. I was scarcely outside the door before I heard him at the typewriter again.'

'An artist has to work,' the Doctor said. 'Still, when a man seems driven . . . '

Bernard leaned across the table toward the other two. 'I have done some asking around. No one knows anything of this place where M. Gastion is supposed to have been raised.'

'Do you think he is an impostor?' The abbé could not help feeling afraid, without knowing exactly what it was he feared. Since he had first gone to the house with the American woman, he had been uneasy. He had told himself over and over that he was being foolish, but that had done nothing to lessen his uneasiness.

'I think . . . nothing,' M. Bernard said, finishing his wine. 'Only, I have talked to different friends in Paris. No one knows anything about this book business of his either.'

He stood up, belching. 'I tell you,' he said, wagging a finger, 'all of the devils are not in hell. If you had seen my poor dogs . . . '

The Doctor rose with him, and with nods all around, he and Bernard left. When they had gone, the abbé sat weighing his thoughts. He wished he knew what he ought to do. He had thought perhaps to tell some of his thoughts to M. Lewis yesterday, but he had known almost at once that the man was too preoccupied.

No, he thought after a moment, it was not merely preoccupation. M. Lewis had changed, just as his wife had. When he had last seen her, she appeared to be beside herself, distracted. He could not even think of the word he wanted to use. And now, M. Lewis had the same unnatural air about him. It wasn't only that he was absorbed in his work. The abbé was used to seeing men who were absorbed. When a man dedicated himself to work, there was a certain nobility to it, but M. Lewis had seemed almost furtive in his absorption.

Possessed. That was the word that had been eluding him. The Lewises acted like people who were possessed.

He finished his drink. The sisters would give him scolding looks if they knew he had had it, and he was very careful in wiping off his lips with his sleeve.

M. Lewis had said yesterday that his wife was returning, and that she was bringing her sister with her, and Madame Lewis had said in the past that her sister was bright and very levelheaded. Perhaps she would be the one to perceive the difficulty and set it straight.

Whatever the difficulty was, the abbé thought uneasily.

20

O villain, villain, smiling, damned villain!
—William Shakespeare

Emily hardly knew what she expected when she arrived in the south of France. With any journey, there was a feeling of expectancy, however muted, but on this journey it was more a sense of foreboding. She could not put it into concrete words, but she wished she could avoid coming here.

At the same time, she was puzzled and deeply concerned. She was at a loss to understand the changes in her sister, and she felt that the explanation must lie here, in this house. It was for this reason alone that she put aside her hesitancy and made this trip, the very thought of which chilled her heart.

Elliot met them at the airport. Emily was shocked to see him. Like his wife, he too had changed, but the changes in him were more physical. He had lost weight, and he had a drawn look, as if some essence of life had been drained from him, as if he was somehow less alive than he had been before.

'What morbid fancies,' she chided herself as she embraced him, but the thought persisted, and the feeling of gloom only deepened within her.

'The house is almost finished,' Elliot said when they were in the car. 'I wish you were seeing it completed, though. It's going to be sensational.'

It occurred to Emily that they had been telling her in their letters for quite some time now that the house was 'almost finished.' She would have thought it done by now.

'It sounds as if you're hinting I go away and come again later,' she said aloud.

Elliot laughed and said, 'Not a chance. We're both delighted you're here at last, aren't we, darling?'

'I would have had no peace if she hadn't come,' Irene said. She had a distracted air, and glancing at her, Emily realized she was only barely aware of their presence. She stared straight ahead through the windshield, and from time to time ran her tongue nervously over her lips.

'She's dying of impatience,' Emily thought.

It was not eagerness to be with Elliot again, however, because she was scarcely interested in the fact that he was beside her in the car. No, whatever she was longing for, she had not yet come to it.

The house, Emily wondered? It was a mystery how Irene's attitude regarding the house could change so profoundly and so suddenly. One minute she hated it, and then she loved it, only to hate it again. Emily had puzzled over it at night until her head ached, and she was no closer to understanding than she had ever been.

Coming up the drive, Emily studied the approaching structure. It was a handsome house, hardly on the order of the grand châteaux of France — they were, after all, only a short driving time from Sully-sur-Loire, or Chinon — but it was no ordinary country cottage either. Of course, it was surely a far cry from what it had been when Elliot and Irene had first seen it and described it to her. The restoration of the exterior was virtually complete now, and she saw the house as it would have looked to those approaching it during its heyday, two hundred years before.

Elliot stopped the car in front and they got out. 'Isn't it great?' he asked excitedly.

'It's beautiful,' Emily said sincerely.

'When I think of our gloomy flat in New York,' he said, turning to unload their bags.

Irene had hardly paused with them. She ran toward the front door and disappeared inside, leaving Emily to find her own way in, or wait for Elliot.

Emily had all but forgotten that there was someone else staying in the house. Irene had not mentioned their houseguest for several days now, but when Emily came into the foyer, she saw a man with Irene, and remembered.

The entryway was shadowy. She thought that the two moved somewhat apart as she stepped inside, but it was difficult to say for certain.

'Here you are,' Irene said, coming forward. 'Philippe, this is my sister. Philippe has been dying to meet you.'

It was only with an effort that Emily managed to continue to smile during the introduction. Never had she met anyone who so revolted her at first glance. She could hardly bear to have him touch her and take her hand, which he kissed in a courtly manner. It was not that he was ugly — in a somewhat gross manner, he might even have been regarded as good-looking — but there was something about him, an aura almost, of evil and filth and animal instincts. His smile was not a smile at all, but a leer, his every touch an insinuation.

The feeling of aversion that she had toward M. Gastion, however, was as nothing compared to the shock yet awaiting her.

Elliot came in after a moment, carrying the bags, which he deposited inside the door. 'I'll take care of these later,' he said, 'Right now, let's have a tour of the place.'

'I'd love it,' Emily said, forcing a show of enthusiasm.

'This is our true pride and joy,' Elliot said, leading her toward an open archway. 'The great hall.'

They came into what had been originally the social center of the house. The restoration of the hall was complete. Across one end was the gallery, with the hanging urns beneath it. The walls had been whitewashed and they gleamed faintly in the afternoon light that spilled through the high windows. At the opposite end was a huge fireplace.

At first glance, the effect was splendid, and, instinctively, Emily murmured 'Magnificent,' but when she had gone down the shallow steps, and turned toward the fireplace wall, she gave an involuntary gasp. Her eyes went at once to the glass painting. It too had been restored and returned to its place above the fireplace, where now the light fell full upon it.

Never in her life had she looked upon anything so horrible, so truly obscene. The effect of the oil upon glass was to give the picture a luminosity that made it literally glow with life. One could almost feel the bruised skin of the helpless victim being dragged through the brush, could all but smell the scent of bruised flesh and flowing blood.

There was something more, though, even more terrible. She looked from the face of the tortured victim, to the face of the man in the painting. He was smiling, a wicked, vicious leer. She had seen that same expression only minutes before, in the face of M. Gastion. The face that looked out of the glass at her, his eyes seeming to look straight into hers, might have been the twin of Philippe Gastion!

She did not know how long she stood in horrified silence, staring up at the painting, but her reaction to it must have shown on her face, because Irene gave a little laugh and squeezed her hand.

'I know,' she said, 'I felt exactly the same thing when I first saw it, but when you've gotten used to it, you'll feel differently. It's really quite singular.'

'So is death,' Emily murmured, forcing her eyes from the painting.

21

I had so worked upon my imagination as really to believe that about the whole mansion and domain there hung an atmosphere peculiar to themselves and their immediate vicinity — an atmosphere which had no affinity with the air of heaven, but which had reeked up from the decayed trees, and the gray wall, and the silent tarn . . .
—Edgar Allan Poe

Whatever elegance or charm the house might otherwise have possessed was spoiled for Emily by the sight of that glass painting. She could take her eyes from it, but she could not remove the sight of it from her mind. It lingered before her wherever she looked, and its mood of evil pervaded the entire house. She followed Elliot from room to room, trying to show enthusiasm as he pointed out each feature and described how the restoration had been accomplished, but she could not help hating the place.

After a time, she realized that Elliot's enthusiasm had waned. She had been so preoccupied with her own gloomy reactions to the house that she had been unaware that he too was preoccupied. Although he still talked at length of each room and each feature, his heart was elsewhere.

At first, she thought it must be Irene. She, surprisingly, had not come along on the tour but had insisted that she wanted to go to her room and freshen up.

'I suppose you're insanely happy to have Irene back,' Emily said offhandedly.

'What? Oh, yes,' Elliot said. He gave her a sheepish glance. 'To tell the truth, I've been so terribly busy, what with work on the house and a new book I'm working on.'

'Elliot, really?' She stopped and put a hand on his arm. 'That's wonderful. What's it about?'

'I can't tell you,' he said. 'I want to surprise everyone, but I'll say this, it's the best thing I've ever done, bar none.'

'How exciting.' She was genuinely thrilled with his news. She had read some of his earlier attempts at writing, and though they seemed to her to lack the polish that comes from practice, she had discerned what she thought was a genuine talent, which she had always hoped he would develop.

'M. Gastion has been helping me with it. He's quite a brilliant man, and he knows a great deal about the writing profession. He's convinced we can get this published as soon as I've finished it.'

Emily did not reply. She had wondered how Elliot thought of M. Gastion, but apparently, Elliot had been charmed by him as well. She could not comprehend how either of these people, whom she thought she knew intimately, could bear the company of a man of his sort.

She tried to be charitable. 'Perhaps he is very charming when one gets to know him,' she said to herself, but with no conviction.

★   ★   ★

While Irene had been gone, Elliot had engaged a woman, a widow by the name of Madame Lafère, to cook for them.

'She can't stay over,' he explained while they had cocktails in the great hall, 'so we have to have our dinners fairly early, but I've had a trial run, so to speak, and her food's very good.'

They had dressed for dinner, and Elliot had invited the abbé up from town. Emily found him a very interesting companion, not so provincial as one might expect, and quite witty in an understated fashion. She was relieved too that his company allowed her to avoid to a great extent conversation with M. Gastion. Nor could she bring herself to look upon the glass painting, but stood so that her back was to it.

'I've known Madame Lafère many years,' the abbé said. 'She is a fine cook, and a good Christian woman.'

'Both qualities are so rare,' M. Gastion said, 'that I wonder how you found them combined in one creature.'

Emily saw that the abbé did not much appreciate this remark. She sensed that he and M. Gastion did not like one another, and she made a decision to discuss the houseguest with the abbé at the first opportunity. Perhaps he could shed some light on the man's mysterious presence here, especially now that the restoration was to all intents and purposes finished. There had been nothing to suggest that he would be leaving anytime soon.

'I do not know that goodness is so rare,' the abbé said. 'We have, for example, our lovely lady from California. From all that I have heard of her, she is certainly good.'

Emily laughed modestly and said, 'I am no angel, Father, if you have any illusions of that sort.'

'I am sure he is right about your goodness,' M. Gastion said. 'It is true, you are good, anyone can see it.' He hesitated, and added thoughtfully, 'And yet, I cannot help but wonder about that other creature, the other Emily. I look forward to meeting her as well.'

'The other Emily? I'm afraid there is only one of me,' she said.

'M. Gastion has a theory that within each of us lurks another self,' the abbé said, in a voice that suggested he did not entirely approve of the theory. 'A dark creature, a hiding man, as it were, waiting to do evil, and to take over in our lives at the right moment. Or should I say, the wrong moment.'

'I'm afraid that whoever he is, he failed to visit me,' Emily said firmly. 'I'm quite sure there is no one lurking inside me.' Her no-nonsense reply seemed to amuse the abbé.

'Might he not have gotten there unobserved?' M. Gastion asked.

'Perhaps, but I can tell you that if I came into my room and found someone who had no business being there, I should order him out at once, and take steps to ensure that he did not come back. It is true, we have to guard against intruders, but we do have that authority.'

M. Gastion smiled and emptied his cocktail glass, and Madam Lafère came in to say that dinner was ready.

The abbé went into the dining room with Emily. He was interested in her confidence in her own powers and her authority over the 'other self' that M. Gastion spoke of. The abbé was a man of abiding religious convictions and yet he could not but admit that he had at times in his life felt the presence of another self within him. Despite piety and prayer and years of devotion to the Church, he could still feel at times as if there were a wild man within him, urging him to do things that his conscious mind did not want to do. At such times, he struggled to exercise his authority, and generally he succeeded, but he did not evict that darker self from his mind. It only went into hiding, awaiting another opportunity to assert itself.

Was he, the abbé wondered, a permanent guest in the household of the mind? Were the rooms of one's mental house haunted eternally by that dark shadow of Satan — for that, surely, was the name of M. Gastion's 'hiding man.'

*   *   *

Later, when they had eaten, and the abbé had left for the village, Emily retired to her room. She was tired, more from the mental strain of the household's peculiarities than from the trip, but she was restless and not yet ready for sleep. She wished for something to read, and remembering that there were already a few books in the library, she put on a robe and started down.

On the stairs, however, she was attracted by the sound of a typewriter, and she came upon Elliot in the room that he had made into a study for himself. He was so absorbed in his work that he was unaware she had come into the room.

She paused inside the doorway and observed him for a moment or two, struck again by his drawn look. Although he had filled the role of host at dinner and kept up his end of the conversation, he had clearly been distracted throughout the evening. After a while, she had guessed that he was eager to be back at his manuscript. Now she saw that he was completely absorbed in it.

That should have pleased her, since she was truly eager to see him achieve success in his writing. Yet there was something about the sight of him just now that only increased her uneasiness. He sat hunched forward, his eyes staring at the paper. He did not look — how traitorous she thought, even to use this phrase — he did not look quite normal. There was a feverish quality about the way he was working that she had never seen before.

She stood at the door, thinking he would notice her, but he never did. There might have been a solid wall between them, so oblivious to her did he remain. At last, reluctant to intrude, she slipped away. She did not go for a book after all, but made her way up the stairs again.

She hesitated outside the door to Irene's room, not knowing if Irene would be awake or not. It struck her as odd that husband and wife were not together on this first night after a separation of some weeks. In the past, despite their tendency to quarrel, whenever they had been apart more than a day or two, their reunions were almost embarrassingly passionate. She could not help but notice that their manner toward one another today had been quite nonchalant.

She tapped at the door lightly and

then, so as not to disturb her sister if she were asleep, opened the door and glanced in.

Irene was in bed, but she was sitting up, stroking the fur of a large, black cat. She smiled at Emily.

Emily gasped with surprise. 'That cat, it's the same one that came to the cottage in Big Sur.'

Irene laughed. 'Really, Emily, you are peculiar at times. How could this be the same cat?'

Emily saw at once that Irene was right, the idea was preposterous, but this cat looked so completely identical.

'You're right, of course, but he does look the same. I didn't know you had a cat.'

Irene stroked the animal's sleek back. Even from the doorway, Emily could hear his purr of pleasure. 'He comes and goes as it suits him. He's quite beautiful, isn't he?'

'I suppose so, if you like cats,' Emily said. She was a trifle disconcerted. She would not have said so aloud, but there was something that disturbed her in the way the cat stared at her with those yellow eyes of his. They reminded her of something or someone, but she could not say just what. She was a little put out, too, at hearing Irene say that she was peculiar. That was the pot calling the kettle black, wasn't it?

'Elliot's working on his manuscript,' she said. 'I saw him just now in his workroom.'

'Yes, I know,' Irene said. If she was jealous of her husband's absorption in his work, she did not show it. She seemed quite content to spend her first evening back in the company of the black cat, who looked as if he had settled down for the evening.

'Well, I think I'll go to bed,' Emily said after an awkward pause.

'Good night,' Irene said, smiling sweet. She seemed to be secretly amused by something. Emily had the unpleasant feeling her sister had been laughing inwardly at her.

22

When you loved me I gave you the whole sun and stars to play with. I gave you eternity in a single moment, strength of the mountains in one clasp of your arms, and the volume of all the seas in one impulse of your soul . . . We possessed all the universe together; and you ask me to give you my scanty wages as well. I have given you the greatest of all things; and you ask me to give you little things. I gave you your own soul; you ask me for my body as a plaything. Was it not enough? Was it not enough?
—George Bernard Shaw

The striking difference in the relationship between Irene and Elliot was made even more apparent to Emily the following day.

'It's a good thing we got back when we did,' she said at breakfast, 'you'd have had to postpone the celebration for once.'

Elliot, even more preoccupied than the

day before, asked innocently, 'What celebration?'

Emily turned to her sister. 'Isn't that just like a man? He's completely forgotten.'

'I'm afraid I must have forgotten, too,' Irene said. 'I have no idea what celebration you mean.'

At first Emily thought they must be joking, but it was obvious they were both honestly puzzled. Feeling a little foolish, she said, 'Hasn't either of you noticed the date? Today is your anniversary.'

They were both incredulous, and then a little flustered, and there was a great deal of laughing and teasing, but the incident served more than ever to convince Emily that something was seriously amiss. Never since their marriage had they forgotten an anniversary.

In New York, they had each year celebrated not only the date of their marriage, but the anniversary of their first meeting as well. She had often teased them about the fuss they made over these dates, and secretly envied them. She could hardly believe that, in so short a span of time, they could have forgotten them.

'Dates, after all, are not important,' M. Gastion said, with what might have been a smirk. 'It is the relationship that matters.'

★ ★ ★

The Michelin Guide recommended a restaurant in a nearby town. Elliot made reservations for dinner, and when he came back from town later, he brought Irene several little gifts of perfume and handmade lace.

'It seems criminal, running off and leaving you on your own like this, the very day after your arrival,' Irene said. 'Perhaps you ought to come with us.'

She was smiling in such a way to make this a joke, and Emily laughed, but again she could not quite accept things at face value. It seemed to her that there was some secret source of amusement that Irene was not sharing — except, Emily amended, with M. Gastion. She saw them exchange a glance that conveyed some secret understanding.

'You are being paranoid,' she said to herself sternly, but despite her efforts to dissuade herself otherwise, and despite the couple's display of affection and jollity toward one another, Emily could not help thinking that the entire anniversary celebration was peculiar.

It was more than the fact that both of them had forgotten it was their anniversary — their temporarily unsettled way of life could perhaps account for that. It was . . . but she could not quite put her finger on it. Elliot made elaborate plans, and Irene took great pains in making ready for the evening, and yet Emily was convinced that neither of them had their heart in it.

★　★　★

Irene came to Emily's bedroom to ask Emily to help her with a clasp. She pirouetted before the mirror there. 'Do you think I'm still beautiful?'

'Yes,' Emily said, 'but in a different way from what you used to be. There's something in your eyes, and your smile: a certain mysteriousness. I'm sure a man would find it frightfully attractive.'

Irene looked into the mirror again. It was true. She had not really even needed to ask. She knew she was beautiful. She had always known that. She thought of Emily, and her love for Elliot, and wondered if Emily suffered anguish when she compared her own plain good looks to this dazzling beauty.

Elliot came in just then, pausing in the door. His glance passed only lightly over Emily and came to rest upon his wife. Despite the years of their marriage, his pulse quickened at the sight of her. He too thought she had never looked more beautiful. Her eyes had acquired an inner light that both fascinated and disturbed him, and her enigmatic smile tantalized him. Not since the first early days of their courtship had he felt such burning desire for her.

'Do I look all right?' she asked.

He laughed and came to where she was standing, and took her in his arms.

'You're wearing a new perfume,' he said. The unfamiliar scent was strange, almost acrid. It hinted somehow of the Orient, of things unknown to him, and mysterious. It was not unpleasant, exactly.

'You haven't kissed me,' Irene said.

She said it to taunt Emily, and even without looking she could guess that a shadow of unhappiness would cross her sister's face. She drew Elliot toward her, and when their lips met, it was not in the restrained, affectionate kiss of a couple that had been married several years, but a kiss of almost intolerable passion. Her lips were like fire to Elliot's mouth.

It was Emily who, after a lengthy time, brought them back to the present by saying flippantly, 'If you order steaks this evening, have them brought to the table raw. They'll cook in no time.'

Irene gave a low chuckle and looked past Elliot at Emily.

Emily was smiling, but her smile faded at Irene's look. She had been unhappy, and despite her affection for both of them, it invariably caused her a twinge of pain to see these two express their love for one another. Always, she tried to make the best of it, but her unhappiness gave her a sensitivity to others' feelings, and she could not help now but see the malicious hatred in Irene's eyes.

She was startled and frightened. What had she done? Had Irene somehow guessed her secret? Even if she had, surely she must realize that Emily's love was something she would never act upon.

'We had better go,' Irene said. Elliot looked like he was dazed. She took his hand and with a brief little nod toward Emily, led him from the room as she might lead a sleepwalker.

Emily followed them to the door and closed it after them. As they walked along the hall, Irene seemed in her mind to hear Emily's unhappy sobs. She thought of Emily alone in her room all evening, crying.

She was delighted.

★   ★   ★

The restaurant they went to was a charming little one in the next town. Despite the unpretentious setting, it was well known and frequented by the fashionable set. The room was crowded, and Elliot was

215

glad he had thought to reserve a table in advance. As they made their way to the table, he caught any number of people turning their heads to stare at Irene. It was obviously a well-to-do crowd, people of money, and some of taste as well, and it was flattering to see how dazzled they were by Irene's appearance.

Irene had never been in better spirits. They had champagne and talked of all sorts of things.

They reminisced of the years they had been married, of little scenes they had shared, even of some awkward moments that were now merely amusing.

At times of late, Irene had been distracted, but now she turned all of her considerable charm on him, and Elliot was as bewitched by her as he had been when they first met. He put aside his customary reserve and responded joyfully to her mood of animation.

He had initially felt reluctant to come tonight, and had made his plans more out of a sense of obligation than from any anticipated pleasure, but he could not be happier that he had done so. Perhaps he had simply been too wrapped up in their house. Now that he was away from it for the evening, he felt as if some weight had been lifted from his shoulders.

After dinner they had cognac. When it was brought, he raised his glass and said, 'Let's drink to us, to our happiness.' They touched glasses. 'It's incredible, how happy I really am. Everything is going so well. The house is all but finished. We could have a party next week if we wanted. I'm at work and well into this new book, and it's the best thing I've ever done. I'm certain it will be a success.'

'You have Philippe to thank for everything.'

'I suppose so, yes.' He frowned briefly, but he was in too high spirits to let anything mar his mood, and in a moment his smile was back. 'And most of all, I have you. I'm so happy, I'm afraid.'

'Afraid? What on earth are you afraid of?'

'Of being too happy. I feel I ought to suffer a little to make up for my happiness. I ought to lose something of value, to propitiate the gods.'

She laughed and put out her hand to his. For a while she did not say anything, and when she did it was to suggest that they go for a stroll.

'Maybe we should be getting back,' he said.

'Oh, why hurry? We so seldom get away together. Let's make an evening of it, why don't we? And Philippe will see that Emily is not lonely.'

He was happy to do as she suggested, and they had their stroll. The village was not much different from the one near their house. Irene looked at the people going by — simple peasant types, ordinary people who lived ordinary lives, praising and sometimes cursing God. She found them highly amusing. She considered herself above them.

Later, in the car on the way home, Elliot said, 'I just want to tell you, you've made me very happy tonight.'

She turned to look at him in the light from the dashboard. 'Do you love me very much?'

He was always a little flustered by direct emotion, but he stammered, 'Very much. Why do you ask?'

'I just wondered.' She leaned back in her seat, putting her head far back as if to go to sleep. She said nothing more for the rest of the drive back.

23

Take heed o' the foul fiend.
—William Shakespeare

It had been an evening of considerable strain for Emily. That fleeting glimpse of hatred she had seen in Irene's eyes had completely unnerved her. Surely she must have imagined it, as she had seemed to imagine so much that was secretive and unpleasant since she had arrived here. She could not quite convince herself, though, that it was only her imagination at work.

She could think of no reason why her sister, who had loved her in the past and whom she still loved with a deep affection, should so change her feelings. The only possible explanation was that Irene might have guessed her secret love for Elliot.

She remembered the photograph she had left up in her bedroom. Would its significance have been so apparent? And even assuming that Irene had, perhaps intuitively, guessed the truth, did it justify such hatred? Emily had never behaved toward Elliot in any way that could possibly have been construed as other than friendship. Surely she could not help her deeper feelings, but her actions had been blameless. Although she rejected pity, her own or anyone else's, she could still say to herself that, if anything, she deserved pity rather than censure. How could Irene, who had everything after all — Elliot, beauty, the love of friends and relatives — resent her for an unhappy passion?

It was surely impossible that Irene could be so unjust, and she tried to reject the entire line of thinking, but it lingered in her mind like a dull ache that would not quite go away.

She had intended to spend the evening in her room. She was not hungry and, more to the point, she had been all too aware that with Elliot and Irene out for dinner, she was left to the company of that awful M. Gastion.

To her surprise, he tapped on the door of her room shortly before the dinner hour, to ask if she would be joining him.

He acted for all the world as if he were the host here, and she his guest. His manner annoyed her, especially since he seemed to be mocking her. He almost seemed to expect her to decline his invitation, and she thought he would merely laugh if she said she was staying in her room.

She had an independent spirit, and she was stubborn and now she would not let him have the satisfaction of thinking that he had intimidated her into hiding in her room, and when he asked if he would have the honor of her company at dinner, she said firmly, 'Of course. I was about to dress to come down.'

When he had gone, however, she regretted her decision. She began to dress as she would to please a date, but when she found herself examining how the dress displayed her figure, she blushed at her reflection in the mirror, and quickly changed into the most somber outfit she had brought along, a plain gray tailored suit that she wore for the most serious business occasions. She pulled her hair back severely and made herself look paler than usual with her makeup. When she finally came down to the dining room, she thought that she looked like someone's old-maid aunt.

'I was beginning to think you had changed your mind and decided to stay in your room,' he said, rising and coming to escort her to her chair.

'Am I late?' she asked, suppressing a slight shudder when his hand brushed her shoulder. She knew very well that she was.

He only chuckled. 'It is a coquettish habit that women have.'

She was prevented from replying because Madame Lafère began serving dinner almost at once. Emily was furious he should even suggest she was flirting with him.

Of course, *he* was trying to be flirtatious, offhandedly, but there was something horribly suggestive in his manner, as if he had some claim to her. Although she continued to turn a cold shoulder to him, he treated her as if he possessed her, as if — she did not even want to think such a thing, but the thought came unbidden — as if he were her lover.

She was struck again by the fact that he was playing the role of host here. He had been doing this since she and Irene had arrived from the airport. Even toward Irene and Elliot, he played the role of the master of the house. She wondered if they were aware of this attitude of his. Now that she looked at things more carefully, she thought an outsider would at once assume that M. Gastion was master here, and the Lewises only guests of his.

'They must be unpleasant thoughts,' M. Gastion said, 'if they make you scowl like that.'

'I was just thinking that you act as if you owned this house.'

M. Gastion laughed, throwing back his head. His laugh was so Mephistophelean she could not help but shiver at the sound of it.

He did not answer her directly, but said, 'Don't you think the house suits me?'

In fact, it did suit him exactly. His style

of dress, his manners, everything about him belonged to an earlier period. He was perfectly at home in this old house. To herself it was still a curiosity, and Irene and Elliot walked about like it was new to them, but M. Gastion might have lived all his life here. He was as suited to the place as the urns in the great hall, or the tiles on the terrace.

She excused herself at once after dinner. She did not much care if he thought she was afraid of him — she was. She could no longer sit and suffer his insinuating glances, and she was terrified to think that he might take her hand to escort her to the hall. She jumped up before he could even come around to hand her out of her chair, and with a breathless apology, fled up the stairs.

Later, when she was in her nightdress and ready for bed, she heard his steps in the corridor outside. She caught her breath when he stopped just outside her door.

He did not come in. The house seemed to sit with breath held, waiting for something to happen. The silence grew heavy.

Her nerves were stretched taut. Still, nothing happened. For what might have been hours she did not move a muscle.

At last she could bear no more of this cat-and-mouse game and, leaping up from the chair in which she sat, she went quickly to the door and threw it open.

The corridor was empty. She stepped into it and looked up and down, but he was nowhere to be seen. He had gone without making a sound.

Something moved in the shadows at the far end of the hall, and for a moment her heart leaped into her throat, but it was only the black cat. It started to come in her direction, but the sight of it only served to remind her of the estrangement between herself and Irene. She went back into her room and closed the door firmly.

She huddled in her chair, terrified, waiting for the sound of Irene and Elliot's return.

24

Eagerly I wished the morrow.
—Edgar Allan Poe

Emily hardly slept that night. She would certainly have locked herself in, however foolish that appeared, but she discovered there was no lock on her door. She told herself that M. Gastion would not come past her room again, that he too had retired for the night, but she started up at every sound in the corridor.

She heard Elliot and Irene come in later, and if it had been any other night but their anniversary, she would have put on a robe and joined them for some late night coffee, but she knew that tonight they would not welcome her company and, instead, she remained huddled in her chair, sleepless and miserable.

By morning, her feelings of uneasiness had deepened into a profound depression. She could hardly manage to keep up conversation at breakfast, and for once was glad that Elliot was again preoccupied with thoughts of his book. Irene and M. Gastion talked back and forth breezily.

Restless, she decided after breakfast that she needed to get out of the house. It was not a long distance into town and she was accustomed to long walks. She decided to stroll into the village.

It was a charming town, not much different from a number of others she knew of in the same general area. She strolled about for a while, happy just to be free of the oddly depressing atmosphere of the house. She would like to have packed her bags at once and left for Paris. She could not even flatter herself that it would upset Irene and Elliot. She almost felt they would be relieved to see her go.

'Then why don't I?' she asked herself, but it was only rhetorical. She knew she could not leave, not so long as her sister continued to behave so oddly. There was something wrong in that house, some mystery that she wanted to settle in her mind. It would only haunt her if she went away.

She was quite surprised, as she strolled along the town's main street, to hear someone call her name. Surely she knew no one here. She turned and saw the abbé hurrying after her.

'I saw you go by,' he said, out of breath, 'and I thought I would catch you and offer you some coffee.'

'I'd be delighted,' she said, and meant it. With everything else on her mind, she had nearly forgotten the abbé, but it was a wonderful change to see his genuine smile and bask in the warmth of his open and friendly charm.

She accompanied him to the little rectory, next to the church. It was simple, but comfortable, and it seemed to reflect his cheerful disposition. A housekeeper brought them coffee and for some minutes they took up a conversation they had enjoyed at dinner regarding French authors of the nineteenth century.

At length, however, the conversation turned to the Lewises and their new home. 'Your brother-in-law has done a very successful job of restoration,' the abbé said.

'Yes. It's a beautiful place, of course, and yet . . . ' She paused. 'I can't feel comfortable there, to be honest. I wish I could explain. There's something . . . ' She shrugged her shoulders. 'I suppose I'm just out of sorts.'

She thought he would think her silly, but he took her remarks quite seriously. 'So you have felt it too,' he said, nodding his head. 'There is an atmosphere there that it is difficult to put one's finger on. Of course, I have no business even talking of these things, but I cannot help but wonder: what do you think of M. Gastion?'

'I loathe him,' she said with a vehemence that surprised even her. 'Forgive me, I know that isn't charitable, but that man is evil, I feel it inside. There's something about him unlike other men. Who is he, anyway? Where does he come from? Do you know anything about him?'

'No more than you, probably.' He told her the story that M. Gastion had

230

told about himself and, after a moment's hesitation, he told her as well of his conversation with M. Bernard, that indicated M. Gastion's background might be somewhat fictitious.

'But what can it mean?' Emily asked. 'Why should he be here at all, and what can he want?'

'The house, perhaps.'

'But that's preposterous. It belongs to Elliot and Irene, and before that it was empty for years. He has no claim to it. It would be futile. How could he expect to get the house from its present owners?'

The abbé stood. 'I have been meaning to do something for several days. A thought occurred to me recently, but I haven't gotten around to it yet. Will you come with me?'

They left the rectory and went to the church itself. It was cool and dark inside, and at present empty. They went through the sanctuary, to a door that led to stone steps winding downward.

'This is an old church,' he said, leading the way. 'Watch your steps, these stairs are crumbling. We don't use these cellars anymore except for storage.'

In the cellar, the abbé hesitated, then chose one of several doors. He had brought a flashlight down with him, and he shined it inside, looking for something.

'It may take a moment to find what I'm looking for,' he said. 'Ah, here it is, I think. Be so kind as to hold this light for me, please. There, like so.'

He moved several boxes in order to get at something behind them and carried it out into the light. Emily saw that it was a painting. Judging from the frame, it was very old.

He propped it against the wall and, taking the light from her, shined it directly on the painting.

Emily gasped. 'It's M. Gastion,' she exclaimed. The face on the canvas was an exact likeness, even to the smugly insinuating smile that the painter had captured.

'Yes, it looks very like him, doesn't it?'

'But what do you mean? Isn't it him?'

'It hardly could be, could it? This painting is more than fifty years old. It has been here almost that long. I thought

I remembered it in an old inventory. It was given to the church, but quite rightly, in my opinion, it was decided that it was not suitable to hang in the church, or the rectory itself, and it was put down here to rot away. I've been meaning for some time to dig it out and see if it confirmed a suspicion of mine.'

'Who is it, then?'

'The last Marquis de Garac.'

For a moment Emily was stunned into silence. She looked at the painting again. It could not be coincidence. The likeness was too accurate. 'That does make things a bit clearer, then. M. Gastion is a descendant of the de Garacs, who thinks he has a claim to the château.'

The abbé did not answer at once. He gave her the light again and put the painting back into the room he had taken it from.

'That may be the explanation. I pray that it is.'

He would not comment further on this, though she pressed him as they went up the stairs again. 'There are thoughts that might be best left unspoken,' he said when they were outside in the sunlight. 'I ask one favor of you. Say nothing of this until . . . ' He paused, not quite sure how to finish the sentence. ' . . . Until I am a bit clearer in my mind,' he finished lamely.

'But if Elliot and Irene are being duped . . . '

'They might not like being informed of it. At present they seem quite pleased with M. Gastion. I do not think they would be particularly unhappy to discover that he has a connection with the house. And it may be that our secret knowledge is secret power.'

Afterward, strolling home, Emily found herself thinking that he had spoken as if they were engaged in some kind of contest. He had spoken of their secret power . . . but power against what?

25

Lilies that fester
smell far worse than weeds.
—William Shakespeare

In the days that followed, Emily found herself a watcher in the house. She was repulsed by M. Gastion and at the same time he exercised an ugly fascination for her. She did not seek out his company exactly, but she contrived to keep an eye on him.

She watched her sister too, and Elliot. More and more she had the impression that they were somehow under a spell, though she felt foolish even forming such a thought. It was difficult to believe that this was the same couple with whom she'd had cocktails in New York only a few months before.

Irene was like a stranger to her. They saw one another each day, they talked of trivial things, they were polite — but it was like sharing a house with someone whom you did not quite like.

As for Elliot, he might as well have been somewhere else. In fact, he was most of the time: in his thoughts. With each day they saw less and less of him. When he was in their company, he was withdrawn and preoccupied with his manuscript, so that you felt guilty for taking him from it.

It was nearing the end of April. Emily wished she could leave. It was a lovely time to travel. Paris would be at its most appealing. If only she could see her way clear to leave, but she could not help but feel that in some way she was needed here, desperately needed. The abbé seemed to feel the same.

'How fortunate they are to have someone like you, who cares deeply for them,' he said.

'But what can I do?' He only shook his head and looked uncertain.

At last something happened that brought matters to a head. The weather had turned hot. Emily took with ease to the practice of an afternoon nap through the warmest part of the day.

She had been in her room that particular afternoon and had slept briefly. She woke to a distant rumbling of thunder that foretold of a storm to come. She went in search of Irene, meaning to suggest that perhaps they could plan a picnic for the following day.

Elliot was at work. She guessed that Irene was in her room. She knocked at the door, as a matter of custom, and went in without waiting for a reply.

She stopped just inside the door, as immobile as if she had been turned to stone. She could not believe her eyes. Irene was there, all right, but she was not alone, as might be expected. M. Gastion was with her. They were across the room, before the windows, and they were locked in a passionate embrace.

Whether they heard her come in or not, she couldn't say, but they were in no hurry to finish their kiss. They remained as they were for what seemed an eternity. Finally, the kiss ended, and Irene slowly turned to look at her sister.

'Hello,' she said, as casually as if

nothing at all were wrong.

Emily staggered backward as if she had been struck a blow. She had known that Irene was taken with this strange man, and she had sensed that there was something more than a casual interest between them. She had even asked herself if M. Gastion could be Irene's lover, but the idea had been so repulsive to her she had rejected it out of hand.

They both looked utterly unembarrassed at being discovered in so compromising a position. At last, Emily found her voice.

'I'd like to speak to you,' she said to Irene.

'Of course,' Irene said. The two had separated, but M. Gastion made no move to go.

'Alone,' Emily added pointedly.

Irene looked about to object, but M. Gastion silenced her with a gesture. 'I do not mind,' he said, and with a bow to Emily, he went out and closed the door softly after him.

Emily knew that it was a moment that called for diplomacy, but she was too beside herself to keep a rein on her feelings.

'Irene, are you mad?' she demanded.

Irene looked unmoved. 'I don't think so.' Something in her expression, a faintly mocking look, reminded Emily of Gastion.

'Do you mean to say that man is your lover?'

'What does it matter to you if he is or not? Or are you envious?'

'Envious? My God, it sickens me to think that he might touch me. Or you. Irene, I don't know what is going on here, but I beg you to come away with me, at once. I'll explain it to Elliot. No, he should come, too. There's something awful going on here, something . . . '

Irene did not wait for her to finish. 'I shall never leave here. Never.'

'You can't be in love with that horrible creature.'

'But I am. I love him madly. I cannot live without him. I am alive only in his arms.' Emily felt as if the room were spinning. She went to the chair at the dressing table and sat down, resting her head in her hands.

After a minute or two, she asked, 'How long has this been going on?'

'Forever.'

Emily gradually began to regain some measure of calm. 'I cannot condone this, of course,' she said. 'I won't tell Elliot, though I beg you to do so at once, but I cannot stay here and be a party to it, either. I will leave in the morning for Paris.'

She started for the door but before she reached it, Irene spoke to her back.

'Can you be so very angry?' she asked in a quiet voice. 'Can you condemn me for what you have longed to do?'

Emily stopped and looked back. 'I? You must be mad. Do you think I would let that man touch me? I would sooner die.'

Irene smiled, cruelly. 'But if it were Elliot?'

Emily's hand went to her throat. She knew. Somehow, Irene had guessed her secret. The knowledge was plain in her eyes. She could not even deny the charge. 'I — I've done nothing. Nothing at all.'

Irene's face twisted into an ugly sneer. 'In your heart, you've done everything, everything that I have done with Philippe, and more. You have yearned for my husband, you have ached to feel his arms about you, his lips upon yours. You have dreamed of him in your sleep, and spoken his name upon waking. Your flesh has cried out for his flesh. Is your guilt any less than mine?'

Emily could think of nothing to say. What Irene said was true. Despite every effort at self control, she had longed for Elliot, yearned to know his kiss, his touch. Did that make her guilty? Was there no virtue in restraint, in resisting temptation? She had thought so, and yet she could see that in her fantasies, she had committed the very sins for which she condemned Irene.

She gave a cry and ran from the room. Behind her, she heard Irene laugh. It was like the laughter of demons, pursuing her down the corridor.

26

Pray for a brave heart . . .
—Juvenal

Emily approached the evening with trepidation. She could not forget the harsh words that she had exchanged with Irene. That she was leaving the next day she had decided firmly. It was not only the quarrel with Irene: she loathed this place. It was evil, of that she was certain. The very atmosphere of the house reeked with all that was dark and malignant, and Philippe Gastion was a perfect match. She could not bear the sight of him; even the thought of him made her skin crawl.

She did not relish the idea of leaving her sister and Elliot in this house, in the company of that man, but she did not see what she could do about it. She could not force them to leave, and indeed, neither of them showed the slightest desire to. Irene had vowed she would not go, and

Elliot seemed as content to stay as his wife. If he thought of anything anymore other than his book, it was the success of his renovation of the Château Garac. He took pride in the house, and felt gratitude to M. Gastion for his part in restoring it.

More than anything else, her heart went out to Elliot. Not only did he seem to have fallen victim to whatever dark spell lay over this house, but he was being cruelly deceived by the wife he adored.

If Irene and Elliot were in any way the victims of misfortune, however, they did not show that they knew it. Both of them seemed very much as usual during the evening. Madame Lafère served her usual substantial dinner, and although Emily only picked at her food, the others ate heartily. Elliot was withdrawn and contemplative, but he had been so for some time now. As for Irene, she might have forgotten their quarrel altogether, such were the high spirits she displayed. She ate and chattered, keeping up a running stream of conversation that was mostly gossip, more often malicious than not, about the local people.

As the meal drew to its conclusion, Emily faced the unwelcome necessity of informing Elliot of her departure. She could not help but feel that she was leaving him in the lurch.

'I've decided,' she said over coffee, directing her remarks to him, 'that I am going to Paris for a few days, and after that, I will return to California.'

He glanced up at her. 'Oh? We'll be sorry to see you go of course. When did you plan to leave?'

'I'm going tomorrow.' She cast a glance in Irene's direction, but she looked more bored than interested in the conversation. M. Gastion sat silently, his expression unreadable.

'So soon?' Elliot murmured.

There was an awkward pause. Emily waited for him to say something further. Twice, he seemed about to, and then thought better of it. He settled for twirling his spoon thoughtfully in his coffee.

Emily could hardly bear her disappointment. She admitted the truth to herself, that she had hoped he would at least try to dissuade her from going. She would have been gratified to see some sadness or regret in his eyes. Her decision was firm, but it would have pleased her to know that one of them cared about her going. She raised her cup to her lips, but it no longer contained coffee — it was filled with bitter gall.

'If you will excuse me,' Elliot said shortly, standing. 'I want to get back to my manuscript.'

Emily could not help asking, 'Is it so very urgent? You seem obsessed with this particular manuscript.'

'It's the best thing I've ever done, I'm sure of it. M. Gastion is very pleased with it.'

'Still, I can't help thinking it's unhealthy, to be so completely absorbed. Don't you think, for instance, that you are neglecting your wife?' She ignored the cold glance that Irene threw her.

She might as well have been talking in another language, however. Elliot had no idea what she was driving at.

'Irene? Lord, no. She wants me to work at my writing, don't you, darling? Just last night she was saying how much it pleased her to see me hard at work on a book that was sure to succeed.'

Emily looked into her sister's eyes, and saw a glimmer of triumph. 'I'm sure it does please her,' Emily said to Elliot. It was useless. Elliot was bewitched by his wife, as he had always been. Nothing could be easier than for Irene to pull the wool over his trusting eyes.

'Well, I'm going to work,' Elliot said. 'Gastion, would you come with me? There's something I want you to read.'

They left and the women lingered on at the table. In the past, this would have been a comfortable interlude, perhaps occupied with trivial but pleasant talk, or perhaps one of those times of silence that are so comfortable between two people who are used to one another's company. Tonight the very air between them seemed stretched thin.

'Irene,' Emily said, 'I beg you to come away with me. When you're away from here, away from that awful man, you'll feel differently.'

'Away?' Irene threw back her head and

laughed. 'I've already told you, I shall never leave here.'

'But can't you see the wrong in what you're doing? For God's sake, think of Elliot.'

A strange expression came over Irene's face then. She did not reply at once, but sat with her head cocked to one side, as if she were listening to a distant sound.

She got up from her chair so suddenly that she nearly knocked it over backwards. She leaned across the table toward Emily and said, in a low whisper, 'For Elliot's sake, think of God.' With that she went out, leaving Emily to stare bewildered and unhappy after her.

Emily had intended to go up to her room but she decided instead to go into the village and visit the abbé. She felt the need of his soothing company.

★ ★ ★

He did not seem at all surprised to see her. If she hadn't known better, she might almost have thought he had been expecting her.

247

'Come in, come in,' he greeted her warmly, leading her into the little parlor reserved for special visitors.

'I'm not disturbing you?' She had only the vaguest idea of how this man's hours might be filled, or whether his evenings were long with empty hours or all too brief and crowded with numerous obligations.

'Oh, dear, no,' he said, 'I should hate ever to be too busy for a friendly visit. Would you like some wine?'

'Thank you, no,' she said. She sat in one of the big, old-fashioned chairs and glanced around the room. She thought of her own elegant apartment, so different from this threadbare place. No doubt she could furnish this entire room for the abbé with what she had spent last year on a sofa alone.

She saw his eyes had followed hers about the room, and she was embarrassed. 'I've come to say goodbye,' she said.

He looked surprised and, she thought, a little disappointed. 'You are leaving?'

'Yes. I plan to leave for Paris tomorrow.'

'So quickly. Will you not have some wine, please? It is local, and quite pleasant.'

She saw then that he himself very much wanted a glass of wine, and did not want to have one unless she did also. 'Perhaps I will, but only if you will have some with me.'

'Yes, yes, of course.' He quickly poured two glasses of the wine. It was, she found, extremely good, and for a moment they spoke of it, but after a few minutes, they went back to their original subject.

He said, with some reluctance, 'This decision to leave is so abrupt — I cannot help but wonder if something has happened to prompt it.'

She hesitated. She would have liked to pour out the entire story. She felt a need to unburden herself, and she knew that this kindly man would listen sympathetically, but, however angry or disappointed she might be in Irene, she still owed her a certain amount of loyalty.

'Father,' she said, swirling the wine about in her glass, 'there are things that I have no right to speak of.'

'Then do not,' he said, leaning forward

to pat her hand comfortingly. 'I do understand. At least I think I do.' He paused for a moment. 'Your sister has changed a great deal.'

'Yes, that's true.' She wondered if he had also guessed the rest of it.

He got up and began to pace the room. He seemed to be weighing his words very carefully.

'Do not be too harsh with her,' he said. 'I know that it is difficult for you, but I tell you, she may not be able to help herself.'

'But, surely, father, we all can. We are responsible for our actions, are we not?'

'Yes, it is true, we are, and yet . . . ' Again he paused. 'Sometimes we are like the man who pushes a cart down a hill, and then jumps into it as it gets rolling. We are responsible, of course, for getting it started like that, but once we have got it rolling, we cannot stop it with the same ease. We are caught up in something, and we must go on. Our only hope is that finally the cart will arrive at the bottom of the hill and stop of its own accord, and we can get out.'

'One could jump out.'

'That is so, if one has enough courage, enough strength of will. And of course, even that may be quite as dangerous, disastrous, even, as to go on. Who can say?'

She set her glass aside. 'Father, what are you trying to say? Do you think I should stay on at that house?'

He wrung his hands in an agitated manner. 'How can I answer that? I prayed that it would do good, having you there. I feel that you are good, and that is a blessing. There is evil there, in that house, and danger. How could I suggest you stay with that danger?'

'Do you think my sister and her husband are in physical danger there? From M. Gastion?'

'There are worse dangers than the physical ones,' he said.

'I don't know whether I should stay, or go.'

He looked at her, hard, as if looking within her, to her very heart. He seemed of a sudden to reach a decision. 'Perhaps after all,' he said, 'it is better if you jump.

Have you a crucifix?'

She shook her head. He went to the writing table against the wall and brought something from it. She took it and saw that it was a tiny cross on a silver chain.

'For tonight, especially, wear this. And stay with your sister. Stay at her side. Tomorrow — tomorrow will be another matter. If everything is still the same — then there are steps we might take.'

'But I don't understand . . . '

'Nor would you if I tried to explain. Wear the crucifix. So long as you have it on, there is no evil great enough to harm you.'

'And my sister? Shouldn't I have a crucifix for her to wear?'

He sighed wearily, and when he spoke, it was as if the words were being forced from him. 'She would never wear it, believe me. If our prayers, and your presence with her, can't protect her . . . ' He shrugged helplessly. 'Stay at her side, all night, please. Tomorrow, if she — tomorrow, try to persuade her to come to see me.'

She knew that the abbé was not saying

all that he wanted to say, but she thought it would be useless to try to argue with him just now. She bade him goodnight, promising him she would remain with Irene for the entire night.

Outside, she saw that the moon was just past being full. It was April thirtieth. It was spring, and everywhere people were shaking off the gray of winter and coming alive to a new season. Here in the south of France it was already hot and sticky.

The clouds that had been filling up the sky moved across the moon, hiding it from sight. In the distance, the thunder rumbled ominously. Despite the warmth of the night, she felt chilled. She started back to the château.

27

This secret dread, and inward horror . . .
—Joseph Addison

The house was strangely dark when she arrived. After a moment she realized it was because it was lit with lamplight now and not electricity. She tried one of the switches, and saw that the power was off. The occurrence was not unusual in the provinces during storms. Madame Lafère had apparently lit lamps about the house before she left for the evening.

In the distance Elliot's typewriter clattered. She smiled ruefully. His world was crumbling in disarray about him and he, oblivious to it, was chained to his typewriter. He seemed as much possessed as Irene did.

She frowned and unconsciously fingered the crucifix the abbé had given her. Possessed? The abbé had spoken of evils, and of danger here. ' . . . There are worse dangers than the physical ones . . . '

Did he think that the house was literally haunted by evil spirits? That seemed so preposterous in this modern era, and yet, it was impossible not to start when a board creaked nearby. And why had he asked her to wear this crucifix?

'Well,' she told herself, starting toward the stairs, 'there is nothing mysterious about that. He is a priest, after all, and this is his symbol.'

Scoffing did not put her at ease, though. She felt the shadows of the house as if they were a weight pressing down upon her. She wished she were already gone from here.

There was a sound below, and she stopped in her ascent of the stairs. Someone was in the great hall. She heard the clink of a glass.

Thinking it might be Irene, she went down again. The abbé had asked her very specifically to stay with Irene for the night. She wondered if he expected something particular to happen. If only he had told her everything. She was certain he had been holding back.

It was not Irene, but M. Gastion in the great hall, having a glass of wine. As she watched, he lifted his glass in a silent toast to the glass painting over the fireplace.

Emily looked at his face in profile. She saw it as a study in evil. He had not yet noticed her, and she made no move to attract his attention. Her eyes went from him to the painting itself.

She gave a little cry and staggered backward as if she had been struck. In a moment, M. Gastion was at her side, trying to put his arms about her. She was filled with horror and revulsion, and stumbled away from him. She pressed herself against the paneled wall and struggled to regain her self-control.

M. Gastion did not attempt to touch her again, but watched her with apparent amusement. She met his mocking eyes, and the hatred he inspired in her helped to calm her somewhat.

'Shall I get you some wine?' he asked after a moment.

She shook her head. She did not yet trust herself to speak.

'You seem to have been frightened badly.'

Still she did not reply. She knew that she would have to turn, would have to gaze once more upon the glass painting, but the very idea filled her with horror. At last she was able to screw up her courage. Slowly she turned her head and looked up at the painting.

It looked normal now, as normal as anything so obscene could look. It was not alive, but only a one-dimensional representation in oil on glass. She looked into the evil face of the man in the painting. The eyes with their odd yellowish cast were focused on some point in infinity — but a moment before, they had been focused upon her! She had looked up, and into those eyes, and had found them watching her!

She gave a sigh and moved away from the wall, putting a hand to her head. Could she have imagined it? She was under a strain, and the kind abbé's words had certainly fired her anxiety.

She had nearly forgotten that M. Gastion was still watching her. His eyes had followed hers to the glass painting and he seemed even more cynically amused.

'You do not seem to like our masterpiece,' he said.

She looked at him coldly. She was struck again by the resemblance between him and the man in the painting. 'It is you, isn't it? You are a de Garac.'

He gave her a little bow. 'At your service. The last Marquis de Garac, Philippe Gastion. You are very clever, mademoiselle.'

'And you have lied to them all this time. Why? Why have you come here? What can you want?'

'Perhaps I wanted to meet you. You are very beautiful, as well as clever.'

His eyes were changed, they were dark and compelling, and something emanated from them, something that went directly into her. She looked away, but almost at once her eyes went, as if of their own accord, back to his.

'Very beautiful.' His voice was lower, caressing. His words were like fingers that softly stroked her body. She felt her hatred for him fade, as the day fades before the approach of night.

'Across the miles and seas, I longed for

you, and spoke your name, and you came,' he whispered. 'You came because your soul heard my call, and answered it. Long before we met, we were together, you and I.'

His voice went on and on, and she was scarcely aware of where she was, or what was happening. She might not have been in the château at all. She might have been on a mountaintop overlooking a rocky valley. She did not so much see this, as feel it, as if a sense beyond sight and sound had taken over her consciousness.

She was dimly aware of physical things. She saw him, as if in a mist, come to where she stood, saw him reach out for her. She knew she was moving into his arms . . .

Suddenly, everything was back to what it had been before. They were standing facing one another in the entryway to the great hall. He jerked his hand back from her as if it had been burned, and stared at her throat with a look of pure loathing.

Her hand went to the crucifix there.

'Why are you wearing that superstitious symbol?' He gave a forced laugh. 'An intelligent, modern woman like you?'

She did not answer. All of the fear, all of her revulsion, swept back over her. She realized that he had been about to touch her, to take her in his arms, and she had offered no resistance. She could not bear to think what might have followed.

She gave a low moan and, turning from him, ran in terror along the hall and up the stairs.

28

A miserable night,
So full of ugly sights, of ghastly dreams.
—William Shakespeare

'What on earth? You look like you've seen a ghost.' Irene turned from her dressing table.

Emily took a deep breath, willing herself calm. 'I've been hurrying. I went for a walk, and to think things out. I've been a little difficult, I think, and when I thought about our quarrel, I practically ran all the way back to tell you how sorry I was.'

Irene looked completely disinterested. She gave a shrug and turning back to her mirror, resumed brushing her hair.

'I wouldn't worry about it.'

'But I do. You know how I hate quarrels, especially those silly ones that go on and on.' It was galling. She was trying hard not to antagonize, trying to humble herself, anything to reestablish a friendly relationship. The abbé had insisted she must spend this night with Irene, and in the morning, persuade Irene to come see him. If she was going to do even the first of these, she had to make up with her sister, however much pride she must swallow to do it.

Unfortunately, Irene appeared altogether uninterested in making up. She said, 'This one could hardly go on and on, could it? You're leaving tomorrow.'

Emily bit her lips. This was going to be even more difficult than she had thought. 'Maybe I was a little impetuous.'

The hand with the brush paused in mid-stroke. 'About what?'

'About going. I really don't want to, certainly not when we've been fighting. Perhaps after all I will stay a little longer.'

'No.' Irene said this with such vehemence that Emily was stunned.

Emily tried to make light of it, but the laugh she gave was dry and unnatural. 'Heavens, it sounds as if you mean to throw me out bodily.'

Irene's haughty manner underwent a change. Her shoulders slumped and she brought the brush down upon the tabletop with a dull thud.

'It would be the last kind thing I could do for you.'

There was something so pathetic in the voice with which she spoke these words that Emily's heart was wrung. She forgot their quarrel, forgot her wounded pride. Nothing was important except that her sister was miserably unhappy. She went to her, throwing her arms about Irene's shoulders in a protective embrace.

'Oh, Irene, I wish I understood all this, but I'm not clever enough. I only know I don't want you unhappy, and I don't want to quarrel with you. Let's strike a bargain, a truce for tonight. I'll stay in here with you and we can put Elliot out in the cold. He deserves it, the way he's been neglecting you for that book, and tomorrow we can . . . '

She felt Irene's body stiffen in her arms, and Irene said again, sharply, 'No.'

'Oh, please!' Emily dropped to her knees. 'No more, Irene, I beg you. I went to the abbé, I talked to him, and he wants . . . '

Irene sprang up, nearly knocking Emily over backward with the suddenness of the move. 'You went to the abbé? You mean you actually talked to him about me, about what I've been doing?'

'I — I needed help. I'm so frightened.'

'You had no right to discuss my business with that old busybody. I hate you for it. And as for your spending the night with me, you must be out of your mind. You know what I do during the night, and I won't want you around. Or did you mean to accompany me to Philippe's room? I've no doubt he would be glad to see you.'

'Oh, Irene.'

'Get out.' Irene pointed dramatically toward the door. 'I'm fed up with this, all your purity and goodness, and looking down your nose at me. I tell you, for the first time in my life, I am alive, I am enjoying myself, and I am doing what I want to do. What do I care if it disgusts you or frightens you? Anyway, you should be happy, shouldn't you? It gives you a chance at Elliot. That's what you've always wanted — you can't deny that.

Well, you can have him. All you have to do is go to him and tell him that I am sleeping with Philippe, and then you can offer him consolation in your arms. You won't be so moralistic then, I'll bet.'

She stopped finally, breathing heavily, her face flushed with her anger. Emily felt utterly defeated. She got wearily to her feet, running a hand over her eyes. As she did so, she remembered the crucifix.

'I'm sorry if I have offended you.' She slipped the chain from her neck. 'Please, at least do just one thing for me. Will you take this and wear it for tonight?'

She handed the crucifix to her sister. Irene took it in her hand, but at once she dropped it as if it had burned her.

'Oh, I hate those things.' She turned her back on it and on Emily.

Emily stooped to pick up the crucifix. For the first time she felt the full horror of Irene's plight. She remembered M. Gastion's reaction to the crucifix, and Irene had reacted the same.

She saw what she hadn't wanted to admit before: Irene and M. Gastion were one. Irene had become the same as that awful man, as coarse and cruel and vulgar.

Emily put the crucifix about her own neck again and stood, but as she was about to go out, Irene spoke.

'After tonight,' she said without turning around, 'none of this will matter.'

'What can you mean?' Emily stood with her hand on the doorknob, but Irene did not answer her or turn. At last, despairing, Emily went out.

29

The Night-Mare Life-in-Death . . .
—Samuel Taylor Coleridge

She went to find Elliot, praying as she went that she would not again encounter M. Gastion.

What a place of terror this house was! She felt beset by shadows of evil. The very air pressed down upon her, threatening to smother her. It took all of her self-control simply to keep from fleeing to her room and barricading herself in it until morning. She was no heroine. Every instinct within her shrank from the horror of this house, of this night, but she must do what she could for Irene, even if Irene did not want her help.

Elliot was still at his typewriter. She paused a moment in the doorway, staring at him. He looked positively feverish in the way he worked, bent over, his eyes glazed and almost unseeing. It was unnatural. Something was in control of him. This was more than the creative impulse of the writer that drove him.

She had a sense of futility. If Elliot too was not himself, what hope was there, what use in trying to talk to him?

The answer was that she must. Somehow she must try to make him see the danger. She squared her shoulders and came into the room, clearing her throat to get his attention. He looked up at her. Despite his wan smile, he looked impatient and displeased to be disturbed.

She did not care about that. She said, 'Elliot, I have to talk to you, at once.'

He made a little palms-up gesture of defeat, and said, 'Well, since you put it so forcefully, I guess I have to listen. What seems to be the trouble?'

'Irene.'

'Oh, yes, that quarrel you had. She never did say what it was about, but I just supposed it would blow over by now. You want me to intervene, I suppose.'

'Elliot, I'm frightened. Irene is in danger here, in this house.'

'Here, in danger? What on earth from?'

He looked amused.

'Oh, Elliot, don't laugh at me. This couldn't be more serious. Please, go up to her, now, and stay with her all night. Stay awake and watch her. I — I can't explain just now, but you must do that.'

He had stopped smiling, but he did not yet look particularly concerned. 'Yes, I can see that you are frightened, but frankly, I think this is all a little silly. How could Irene be in any danger? I mean, from what? Even if there were a herd of hobgoblins on the lawn, there's all of us in here — you and I, and M. Gastion.'

She put a hand on his shoulder. 'No, not him. You — you mustn't let her be alone with that man, not ever. Please keep him away from her, especially tonight.'

His eyes darkened. 'What are you talking about?'

She was frightened of trying to tell him everything. She did not know what his reaction would be to the truth, and now of all times she wanted him calm. 'I don't trust that man,' she said lamely.

'Obviously.' There was an awkward pause. 'Well, even assuming you have some reason to distrust him, let's be reasonable, shall we? I mean, he isn't likely to see her anyway tonight. It's after her bedtime already. And what could he do? If he meant to murder her in her sleep, he could have done so before this. Or do you think he's going to carry her bodily from the house? We're both here, aren't we? If you're that frightened, spend the night with her. I'll sleep down here.'

'I suggested that to her already. She — she refused to let me.'

'There, you see, she thought you were being foolish, too. Your room is right next door, for Pete's sake. Leave your door open. If he comes by with an axe in his hand you'll be sure to hear him.'

'Hear whom?'

The sound of M. Gastion's voice behind her made Emily jump. He stood just inside the room, grinning at her. She had no idea how long he had been standing there, or how much he had heard.

'Emily thinks you're going to murder my wife in her sleep.'

M. Gastion laughed, showing his black

teeth. 'I am, in fact, but how did you find out?'

Elliot found this very funny. He laughed aloud, but he made an effort to suppress his laughter when he saw Emily's face. 'Oh, come on, pet,' he said, patting her hand. 'It's only a joke.'

M. Gastion came across the room. Emily shrank away from him. If he had even tried to touch her, she would not have been able to prevent herself from screaming.

'I came down to see how the manuscript is progressing. I thought we might go over that last part, if you have some time.'

Elliot looked at Emily. 'Do you mind?'

M. Gastion's expression was smug and confident. Wordlessly she turned and left the room, not daring to look back. She heard their voices as she went up the stairs, and some muted laughter. No doubt they were savoring what Elliot regarded as M. Gastion's little joke.

She went to her room. There was nothing more that she could think of to do. Irene would not have her in her room for the night. Elliot would not listen. He thought it all a joke. M. Gastion was in charge here, a puppet master pulling the strings.

Well, she was not yet his puppet. She did not know what she could do against him, but she did not mean simply to go to sleep and let him have his way. She did as Elliot had suggested, and left her door open. She meant to stay awake the entire night, watching.

She might be placing herself in grave danger, but there was one thing that would protect her. M. Gastion was frightened of the crucifix and so was Irene. She did not know why, nor did she care especially. It was not necessary that she understand everything. What mattered was that, so long as she wore the crucifix, he was prevented from working the same sort of spell on her that he had worked on Irene and Elliot. That was her only consolation. It was a slim one, admittedly, but it was all she had, and she clung to it, fingering the crucifix repeatedly.

She changed into her nightgown, and put a robe over it. She made an entry in the appointment book she always carried with her, and was suddenly struck by the date. Something the abbé had said during one of their conversations came back to her. He had spoken of *Walpurgisnacht* — Walpurgis Night, one of the nights sacred to evil. He had spoken of witches and Grand Sabbats, and of Satan, whose ascension was celebrated.

She had paid little attention then and she would not have remembered it at all, except that she had wondered about the date. It fell on the last night of April, and the following day, the Feast of St. Walpurgis, was May first, and she had wondered if there were any connection between this old legend and the modern day use of the term, Mayday, as a warning signal.

Because of that idle question, which had gone unanswered, the date had stuck in her mind as it would not have done otherwise, and now, when she looked at her calendar, she saw that tonight was *Walpurgisnacht*. Earlier this evening the abbé had seemed to attach great importance to this night, and Irene, too, had indicated that this night was significant, as if things were to be resolved before the sun rose again.

If M. Gastion were as evil as she believed him to be, might he choose tonight to do whatever it was he intended to do? It seemed likely.

She brought the chair around so that it faced the door, and sat in it watching. She told herself there was no danger of her falling asleep, for which she could be grateful. She was wide awake with tension and fear, convinced she couldn't have slept if she had wanted to.

Despite this conviction, however, she eventually found herself getting drowsy. The time dragged by. The house lay still about her. She was too far away from the study to hear Elliot's typewriter. There had been no sound from Irene's room since she had come up. No one went by in the hall.

She watched the motes of dust dance in the light of the lamp, and found herself becoming more and more fascinated by their whirling movements. If one used only a little imagination, one could almost think they were forming themselves into shapes . . .

She sat up with a start. She had very nearly fallen asleep watching the dust in the lamplight. Frightened, she got up and began to walk back and forth, running her hands over her arms. It was quite cool now, and she wished there were a fire in the fireplace.

She thought of going down to ask Elliot to build one for her, but she did not want to face M. Gastion again, nor did she want to abandon her post and leave Irene unprotected. It was long past the hour when the cook, Madame Lafère, would have left to go home. There was no one else in the house to whom she could turn.

She went to the window and looked out. The storm that had threatened had begun, although so far it was only a gently falling rain. A thin mist had begun to rise. It crept upward like the fingers of a bony hand.

The cold was really becoming uncomfortable. She went to the armoire and got a sweater, draping it about her shoulders. When she went back to the window, the mist had grown thicker. She could hardly see out, it was so crowded against the window.

At least now she was wide awake again. She settled herself in her chair again, to watch the hall.

Almost at once, she fell asleep.

30

*They cannot die, but must go on
age after age, adding new victims and
multiplying the evils of the world.*
—Bram Stoker

She could hardly say whether she was awake or asleep, or how much of what was in her mind was dreaming. She knew that she was waiting for something, and was very anxious, and at the same time, powerless to act. She felt as if her limbs were made of lead — her hands, her feet, even her brain felt weighted, and when she moved, it was as if in slow motion.

She gradually realized that the air felt oddly heavy and cold, and there was a clinging dampness to it that chilled to the very marrow of the bones.

She opened her eyes, or thought she did in her dream. The room was dark, although she had left the lamp burning. After a moment, she realized it was because the fog had filled the room with its thick clouds. The window was open, and she felt that she should go and close it, but she could not move at all.

She closed her eyes again, but as if she saw right through the lids she saw the mist growing rapidly thicker and thicker, like billowing smoke, swirling about her. It began to take shape, forming itself into a sort of column. Her thoughts whirled with it. She saw a pair of eyes, red and malignant, staring at her from the center of the pillar of mist — watching her, growing larger as they loomed closer and closer. Somehow, her hand lifted, as of its own volition, and her fingers touched the silver of the crucifix.

★   ★   ★

She gave a cry and woke up. Her heart pounded, and for a moment her mind refused to function. She could not think where she was, nor why. She looked around wildly for the familiar evidences of her apartment, and saw instead a room that was unfamiliar and foreboding. The flickering lamplight lent an air of unreality.

Then she remembered, and with memory came a wave of anguish. She had fallen asleep! When she most needed her wits about her, when above all else she needed to be awake and alert, she had slept as easily as a babe in its mother's arms.

The corridor was empty. The entire house was still. Nothing stirred, not even the air about her.

There was something ominous about the stillness. It was as if the house was watching and waiting for something to happen.

She took the lamp and went to the door of Irene's bedroom. It was closed, and she hadn't the courage to go in, knowing she would not be welcome. She listened, but she could hear nothing. Was Elliot there with her? If so, then no harm had been done by her falling asleep. However shortsighted Elliot might be, she knew that he would not stand idly by and allow any direct harm to come to his wife.

But she could hear nothing! She left

the door and went toward the stairs, listening. The sound of Elliot's typewriter did not drift up from below, as it had earlier. She knew that she ought to take comfort from that silence, but somehow she could not.

At the bottom of the stairs she paused, listening again. She could hear the pounding of her heart, and the dry rasp of her breathing. The lamp cast eerie flickering shadows before her, which seemed alternately to beckon and to warn her away. Outside, the storm that had threatened earlier now raged.

The soft fabric of her nightdress made a little whispering sound, as if invisible imps came after her, whispering among themselves. Despite the emptiness and the stillness of the house, she had an impression she was not alone. She imagined a thousand eyes staring at her from each shadow. More than once she thought she saw someone or something move in the darker corners, and lifted her lamp high, only to see that there was no one there.

There was no sound from Elliot's study

and the door was closed. She pushed it open and stepped inside. It was dark within, and at first glance, holding her lamp aloft, she thought the room was empty. Elliot had gone up to bed, then. He was with Irene and there was no need for her to continue her vigil through the rest of the night.

She gave a little sigh of relief and turned to retrace her steps. It would be nice to be able to climb into her own bed and sleep without worrying for whatever was left of the night — but before she could leave, a sound arrested her. It was a low moan, so soft as to be almost a whimper.

There, in the darkness, in what she thought was an empty room, it assaulted her senses. Her skin crawled, and she gave an involuntary shudder.

She lifted the lamp again. At last she saw Elliot. He was lying across his typewriter, his head cradled in his arms, so that it had been very easy to overlook him before. She nearly dropped the lamp. A thousand thoughts crashed into one another in her mind. He was dead! M.

Gastion had killed him. He might even still be in the room, lurking in the shadows, perhaps approaching her from behind, his hands out to her . . .

She turned quickly about in a full circle, her eyes wide with horror, but there was no one creeping up on her.

'You must not panic,' she told herself aloud. She swallowed, her throat dry as dust, and went across the room to where that dark shape lay unmoving across his writing table.

He was not dead. She found a pulse. It was normal. His breathing was even and regular. He seemed quite simply to be sleeping, except that she could not rouse him from his sleep.

'Elliot,' she said, shaking his shoulder; and again, more forcefully, 'Elliot, wake up.'

He slept on, despite her continued efforts. It was the sleep of a man who is drugged. As this truth came home to her, she felt tears singing her eyes.

'Oh, Elliot, please, please wake up,' she cried, shaking him until she nearly made him fall out of the chair onto the floor, but he did not stir.

It was useless. He was drugged or that awful man had put some sort of spell on him.

Irene! The name flashed into her mind again. Whatever M. Gastion was doing, Irene was at the center of his evil schemes — and she had left Irene's room unguarded to come down here.

She turned and ran from the room, along the corridor, her gown making a cloud of white behind her. Up the stairs she raced, one hand holding the lamp, the other clinging to the banister.

She did not pause to knock at Irene's closed door. She ran straight to it and without hesitation threw it open, bursting into the room.

The room was empty. The bed had not been disturbed and a lone lamp burned on the dresser, casting its yellowish glow.

'Irene!' Emily ran from the room. She knew where to look, and although it filled her heart with terror to think of even approaching that man's room, she had not the slightest doubt that Irene was with M. Gastion. Nor did she doubt that her sister was in danger, a danger the significance of which she herself could only guess.

She ran and as she ran she cursed herself a thousand times over for a fool, for having fallen asleep. She had been warned about this night. She had realized it was *Walpurgisnacht*, and tonight of all nights that man would work his evil. How could she have been so careless?

M. Gastion's door was closed. She did not trouble to knock but threw the door open, letting it crash back against the wall, and stepped into the room, holding the lamp before her. She felt as if she were stepping into the very chamber of Satan himself. She dared not think of what might lie before her.

31

Behind the dim unknown,
Standeth God within the shadow . . .
—James Russell Lowell

His room was empty too. She held the lamp high and directed its glow slowly about the entire room, but there was no one here.

'Irene,' she called aloud. She turned around, and around again. Where could they be?

She went into the hall, looking back the way she had come. Not that way, surely, she had just come from there. She went in the other direction, toward the service stairs.

The door stood open at the head of those narrow, twisting stairs. As she paused at the opening, she heard a sound from below, the sound of a door creaking on its hinges.

'Irene,' she cried, starting down, 'wait!'

The stairwell twisted, so that she could see no more than a foot or so before her. She knew that she might at any moment come round one of those curves and find herself face to face with Philippe Gastion. She did not delude herself that he would welcome the sight of her.

She was a coward. She admitted it. She was terrified of this night, of the danger she was rushing to meet. No power in Heaven or earth could make her run down these stairs like this, rushing to meet she knew not what horrors — nothing but the knowledge that Irene was in mortal danger, and needed her. She ran, and as she ran, she prayed. She had no weapons against this evil, except her faith that there was a God and her conviction that good was ultimately greater than evil. She prayed now for some miracle, some source of strength to help her.

The stairs opened into the kitchen. Still there was no sight of anyone.

Had she been wrong? Were they upstairs after all, hiding somewhere? The empty room mocked her frustration.

She heard a sound in the corridor and

ran in that direction. Ahead of her she saw a glimpse of white, disappearing through a door. She had found them! If only she were not too late!

She caught up with them at last on the terrace. The tiles gleamed with wetness from the rain. The falling drops glittered in the glow from the lamp. Across the terrace, M. Gastion was half over the iron railing. Irene waited to be helped over, her hand in his. They were preparing to leap to the ground below, into the brambles and thick underbrush.

'Irene, wait,' Emily cried. The lamp sputtered in the rainfall, and its light danced wildly. Under her breath, Emily prayed again for help from above.

Irene had been about to follow the man in black, but for a second, she hesitated.

'Irene, in the name of God, don't go,' Emily cried.

At last Irene turned to look at her. Her eyes were wide and staring, and they sent a chill through Emily's body. Irene looked like a sleepwalker, as if someone other than herself were in possession of her.

'Emily,' she said softly, 'Emily, darling,

go back inside, please.'

Her voice was so calm, so untroubled, that for a moment Emily was nearly lulled into thinking she had exaggerated the danger in her mind. Perhaps there was nothing more to this than a lovers' tryst.

She gave her head a shake. No, that was only that demon, clouding her thoughts again. Somehow he had the power to enter her mind, to twist her thoughts about — but only if she permitted it. Her mind was her own, and nothing could enter there unless she allowed it access.

She crossed the terrace toward them. Gastion shot her an ugly glance and made a gesture for Irene to come with him. She would have done so, too, but they were not fast enough. Emily grabbed Irene's other hand and yanked her away. His grip was relaxed, and Irene's hand slipped from it.

Irene blinked, as if she were suddenly awakened. Emily half drew her across the terrace, away from the grip of the fiend at the railing. Her sister looked dazed but she allowed herself to be dragged away.

'Come,' Gastion cried in a booming

voice. It was like an electric shock upon Irene. She stopped in her tracks, her body stiffening.

Emily whirled about. Gastion was climbing back over the railing. Emily looked into his face, and for a moment she was struck numb. Never had she seen such frustrated malice. Those horrible eyes seemed to throw out sparks of hellfire, the brows knotted until the folds of skin were like the coils of Medusa's snakes, the mouth twisted viciously. If ever a look could kill, if ever a face meant death, she saw it before her now.

He stumbled a little on the wet surface of the terrace, catching the railing again to regain his balance, and in that moment, she lifted the lamp in her hand and, crying, 'You devil,' she threw it straight into his face.

The glass shattered, and in an instant the oil, bursting into flame, splashed across him. He gave a shriek of pain.

Emily seized Irene's wrist, meaning to run with her, but to her horror, Irene reacted as if it were her face that was aflame. She threw her hands across it and gave a heartrending scream. Then, as if she had been struck with a thunderbolt, she sank into a heap at Emily's feet.

There was a cry from the railing and Emily turned to see Gastion, his hair still smoldering, coming toward her with all the fury of hell in his eyes. So palpable was his hatred that she paled before it and shrank away from him.

'Elliot,' she screamed at the top of her voice. 'Elliot, for God's sake, help me.'

Gastion came toward her, crouched low like an animal preparing to spring. His hands reached out for her, his face twisted into an expression of triumphant evil. She felt his hand on her arm, and it seemed as if all her strength, all her will, fled from her. She thought that she too would sink to the floor in a faint.

At the very second when she would have done so, even as he was dragging her into his arms, she remembered the crucifix. It had fallen within the folds of her gown, but now she seized it in her hand, holding it up for him to see.

At once he let go of her with a cry of rage like a wounded jungle beast. She stumbled backward, screaming again for Elliot. She felt doomed — if that monster came for her again, she would have no strength left to resist him.

It was escape that he wanted now, however. He turned from her and, bending down, seized Irene in his arms. He threw the limp body across his shoulder as if she were a sack of rags, and before Emily could even move to block his path, he had bounded across the terrace and, in one great leap, cleared the railing.

She heard him land in the underbrush below with a crash.

32

*There is a countenance which haunts me,
turn as I will. There is an hysterical laugh
which will forever ring within my ears.*
—Edgar Allan Poe

For a moment there was silence, so awful
a silence that she thought her brain must
burst, that she must surely go mad. Then,
from below, came a sound to break the
silence, a sound so horrible, so inhuman,
that she knew her dreams would be
forever haunted by it.

From out of the darkness below the
terrace came a laugh, a single shriek of
glee. He had won, that monster, and now
he paused to gloat, to signal his victory.

It came and went, and the silence fell
upon her again, but her screams of
horror must have penetrated the depths
of the charmed sleep that Elliot slept, or
else the charm had gone with the man
who cast it, for a moment later, Elliot

appeared in the doorway.

'Emily. Good God, what's going on here?' He looked dazed, his eyes taking in the broken lamp, her terrified appearance, the empty terrace beyond.

'Elliot, oh, thank God.' She ran into his arms, sobbing with relief. 'He's gone. That monster, Gastion. He's taken Irene and run into the woods.'

'Irene? She'd never have gone . . . '

'She was unconscious,' she cried. There wasn't time now to explain the rest, even if he would believe her. 'He took her, over his shoulder . . . '

'But where?'

'Somewhere out there. Someplace evil, I'm sure of that. He jumped over the railing with her.'

Elliot freed himself from her embrace and ran to the railing, looking down. In the distance, he had a glimpse of white, rushing toward the woods.

Like a wave breaking over a rock, the full horror of the moment suddenly rushed over him. He remembered Emily's warning earlier, and one part of his mind had known that she was right, but another part of him had only been amused. He felt as if he had been in a trance, as if he had been standing aside watching someone other than himself play his part in the drama of events, while he was helpless to do anything.

He remembered Gastion's coming to him, remembered the sound of the man's voice, going on and on, talking not about the manuscript at all, but about distant mountains and valleys. It was as if Gastion's voice had actually transported him to another world, had lifted him to high peaks from which he looked down upon the pitiable race of men, like ants, far below.

How long he had dreamed he had no idea, but a moment before, the dream had been shattered. Through the thickest of the mists that encircled his mind, he had heard Irene scream, and the pain of that cry, the urgency of her need for him, had penetrated even the spell that had been cast over him. His love for her had brought him at once back to reality. His mind was his own, and he saw that he had been a fool and a dupe, a slave to that evil's man's wishes.

He cursed himself, but at once realized that more than words were needed now. He turned and raced back toward his study. Emily ran after him.

'What are you going to do?' she cried.

'Go after that devil. If he's harmed Irene, he'll pay for it.' It was an empty challenge, he knew. In his mind's eye, he knew that Irene was already harmed, that the harm had begun long ago, and he had been too blind to see it happening. It was incredible how clearly he could see everything now, as if a curtain had been torn aside that had hidden everything from view before.

He threw open a drawer of his desk and brought out a revolver. He examined the chamber to be certain that it was loaded.

'Stay here,' he said, starting for the door.

'Elliot, no, I beg you, let me come with you. Don't make me stay here alone.'

He was about to argue, but the look of sheer terror on her face silenced him. He nodded wordlessly and she ran behind him.

They went out by the front door and around the house to the spot at the rear where Gastion had emerged from the underbrush. Elliot ran toward the woods, following the direction of that glimpse of white. He knew that had been Irene's gown. He thought of her unconscious form carried through those dark woods, and for some reason he had a vision of the glass painting hanging in the great hall. In his mind he saw the woman in the painting, bleeding where the flesh had been cut by the thorns and brambles, the scarlet staining the white of her flesh. He ran faster, only barely aware of Emily trying to keep up with him.

It seemed as if Gastion had summoned all the forces of night to hinder their pursuit. The storm, which had dwindled to a light rain, suddenly erupted again. Lightning flashed violently, followed almost at once by a clap of thunder. The landscape before them was lighted with an otherworldly glow, and in it they had just a glimpse of the dark figure ahead, Irene's limp body trailing down his back, her hair and her hands dragging upon the ground.

'Gastion, stop,' he yelled, but the thunder swallowed up his words even as the blackness swallowed up the scene. The rain became a torrent, pouring down upon them, slowing them, holding them back.

Emily strained to keep up with Elliot. Her sides ached already with the effort. Once she stumbled and fell, and he went on, oblivious, so that by the time she staggered to her feet again and went after him, he was already several yards ahead of her. It was all she could do to keep him in sight as they plunged into the thickness of the woods.

She was nearly frozen. The rain had long ago soaked her nightgown. She was grateful when they were in the woods and sheltered from the worst of the storm, but the thick growth that sheltered her from wind and rain impeded their progress as well, and hid the pair before them from view.

At one point Elliot stopped, looking about as if he had lost the trail. She stumbled up to him, falling against him breathlessly. As she did so, she caught a glimpse of white ahead and to their left — a piece of Irene's gown that had caught on a branch. She pointed, not even able to manage the breath to speak, and Elliot at once rushed in that direction. It suddenly came to him where they were headed: Gastion was rushing toward the old graveyard. That was where this trail was headed.

Emily stood for a moment, swaying weakly, exhausted. In the next moment, Elliot had disappeared from sight, but a gunshot suddenly rang out, and someone cried in pain.

She took a faltering step, and realized that she was alone in the darkness, in the night, in the thick of the forest. She could not bear it. She was seized with panic. She shrieked and began to run blindly, crashing through the brush, heedless of the blows and cuts inflicted upon her by the tangled growth. Again and again she screamed, running blindly on. She heard Elliot's voice, somewhere in the blackness, calling her name, but she could not tell from what direction it came.

She felt as if all the demons of hell

pursued her. Every leaf that brushed her face was the kiss of some nightmare ghost, each twig a hand that would seize and hold her, and drag her down to hell.

She heard Elliot's voice again, as if through a haze. 'Emily, for God's sake, where are you?'

'Here,' she screamed. 'Elliot, oh, Elliot, help me!'

She had followed her own blind path through the woods, not the more twisting one that Elliot had followed in pursuit of his prey, and her headlong flight through the forest's growth had brought her ahead of him.

She burst into a clearing. The lightning flashed, and she screamed again. She had run right into the path of Gastion. He was there, before her, Irene's body still over his shoulder, his face grotesque with hatred at the sight of her.

33

Death has done all death can.
—Robert Browning

That sight of her tormentor in the lightning flash was like the slap on the face that she needed to check her panic. She stopped so suddenly that she nearly pitched over.

'You,' Gastion roared. He made a snarl like the sound of an angry bull and, throwing Irene's body aside like a rag doll, he rushed at Emily.

There was another shot, this time so close that it left a ringing in her ears. It was a moment before she realized that Elliot had come into the clearing almost directly behind her and had fired past her at Gastion.

The man in black stopped in his tracks, clapping a hand over his shoulder. He looked past her, at Elliot, with a look of pure malevolence. Then he whirled about and as quick as a cat was gone into the brush again.

Elliot came to her, putting an arm about her to steady her. 'Are you all right?' he asked.

She nodded her head weakly and pointed to where Irene lay at the base of an oak tree. Elliot stooping down and turned her over. There was blood on her face. The rain began to wash it away in little rivulets.

'Is she . . . ?' Emily could not bring herself to say the word.

'She's alive,' he said, lifting his wife's limp figure in his arms. 'But just barely. We'll have to take her to the doctor.'

Emily cast a glance in the direction in which M. Gastion had disappeared. 'I'll catch up with him, never fear,' Elliot said grimly. 'There's no place on earth he could go to escape me.'

She was too exhausted to reply, and had she told him what she was thinking — that M. Gastion's refuge might not be of this earth — he would have thought her hysterical. He had started off walking briskly back toward the house, and she hurried after him.

It seemed to take forever to reach the house. She fell behind again and again, and was torn between wanting him to hurry on with Irene, and her fear at being left alone in the woods. Her reasoning mind told her that M. Gastion was not likely to be on their heels just now. She could not hope to understand it clearly, but she thought she had a good idea where he had gone.

Once, she fell, and Elliot, glancing back and seeing her on her knees, started back to help her, but she struggled up, saying, 'It's all right, go on, I'll catch up.'

At last they reached the house. It was the only time that structure had ever looked welcome to her, but they hardly paused there. Elliot went straight to the car and in moments they were speeding down the lane and then along the road toward the village.

Elliot knew the local doctor, Doctor Florimond, only slightly, but he knew the house in which he lived, just at the edge of town. The doctor was long since in bed asleep, his house dark, but Elliot's determined pounding at the door produced lights inside, and a moment later a window opened in the door to reveal a sleepy face peering out.

'What is it?' the man demanded. He looked suspiciously from Elliot to the car beyond, where Emily sat staring out.

'My wife,' Elliot explained breathlessly, 'There's been an accident. I'm afraid . . . '

Something in his voice convinced the Doctor that the emergency was real. The window closed again and a second later the door swung open.

'Bring her in here,' the Doctor said, indicating his parlor.

Elliot bounded back to the car and lifted Irene's still limp body into his arms again. Emily followed him into the little house. She had said nothing at all to him during the drive. She was only beginning to get her breath back, for one thing, and she knew he could not give him the hope he wanted.

She thought that they were too late and that nothing could be done to restore Irene to him. She had felt Irene's pulse as they sped along the road. It was there, but barely discernible. It seemed to her that Irene's skin was already cold and her face was as white as snow except where it was bleeding.

She was sure her sister would not survive. It was horrible and yet, she could not help thinking that this was only the aftershock, as it were. Looking back upon the past few weeks, she saw that Irene had died to them a long time before, and this moment of death was nothing compared to what they had lost previously.

The Doctor wasted no time now in questions. He looked at the pale face, scratched and bleeding from that mad chase through the woods, and went at once for his kit. Emily sat in a chair facing the sofa on which they had laid Irene.

Elliot went to the window and stood with his back to the room, his forehead resting against his hand where he held the casement. He looked despairing and beaten, and Emily wished that she could say or do something to comfort him.

She knew the man she loved was suffering an agony of his own, far worse than the agony of death, and there was nothing she could do to help him. She had seen his face as he drove the car a short time before, and could only guess at the feelings of remorse he was suffering, the self-incrimination. She had never thought him capable of deep emotion before, would never have dreamed him capable of the profound grief she saw in his face.

The Doctor was back in a moment. He wore only a tattered and none-too-clean robe, which he had put on to answer the door, and his legs, protruding from it, looked thin and knobby.

A short round woman in a nightdress followed him into the room — his wife, apparently, and his nurse as well. The two of them began a swift examination of their patient. Elliot turned around but he did not leave his post at the window. Emily sat with her hands in her lap. Her emotions had been too buffeted throughout this awful night. She felt numb.

The Doctor prepared a syringe and gave Irene an injection. His wife had gone out and returned with a basin of steaming water, and she set to work bathing the wounds. She had to tear and cut away the remnants of Irene's gown, which was in shreds.

Throughout all this, Irene lay as if she were already dead. Emily had an urge, which she resisted, to cross the room and cover the poor creature's face, as one does with the deceased. She tried to pray that Irene might live, but somehow she could not find the words. She found herself instead praying for Irene's soul, that she might find peace in another life.

Suddenly there was a soft sound from the sofa, like a sigh. Emily's heart skipped a beat. Irene's hand fluttered slightly, as if to reach out for something. Elliot's face had the pallor of death and it was only with the greatest of efforts he restrained himself from rushing across the room and seizing his wife in his arms.

The Doctor himself seemed startled by this evidence that life lingered. For a second he paused, watching the face before him. In that pause, Irene spoke, faintly and yet distinctly.

'Emily,' she said.

For all that she thought she had given

up hope, Emily was across the room in a single movement, falling on her knees by the couch.

'I'm here, darling,' she sobbed, tears streaming down her cheeks.

Irene's eyes opened. She looked up into her sister's face, and it seemed as though she were trying to smile, but hadn't the strength for that. She did manage to raise one hand, ever so slowly, toward Emily's throat.

Emily had thought that there was no more capacity within her for horror, but she had not dreamed in her wildest imaginings of a moment like this one. It was the point of death for her sister. It was the moment when she ought to forgive Irene and bless her, and when Irene ought to seek forgiveness, and make peace with her God.

Even in this, though, in this most solemn of all moments, the woman on the sofa remained a slave to the horrible monster who had taken over her life.

Through her tears, Emily looked into Irene's eyes, and it was not a plea for forgiveness that she saw there, nor a yearning for peace. It was hatred, malevolent and cruel. It was the look of evil. The eyes that stared upward into hers were his eyes, M. Gastion's! Even now, if she had the strength, Irene would have strangled her, for his sake.

Emily could not help herself, she gave a gasp and shrank back from that grasping hand. It clawed at her, the fingers bent like the talons of some vicious bird. Then, with a final look of pure loathing, Irene closed her eyes and breathed her last.

Silently, Emily said, 'Thank God.'

34

Much is to be done.
—Samuel Johnson

There was nothing more that could be done. Life had fled that broken body. The soul, Emily well knew, had fled long before this. She could scarcely gaze upon the lifeless figure without a feeling of horror, and it was only with the greatest of efforts that she kept this feeling of revulsion hidden from Elliot.

She did not feel she was unfaithful to the memory of her sister. She genuinely mourned Irene's passing, but this empty shell that only minutes before had gazed on her with evil was not Irene. Irene was that lovely, thoughtless, shallow creature who had disappeared some time before, leaving a mocking shadow in her place.

She promised herself that she would keep all this to herself and not add to Elliot's grief. He was suffering enough as it was. Perhaps he would guess the truth. She didn't know, but guessing was not nearly so horrible as true knowledge. So long as he only guessed, there was still the hope for him that it had not been so completely awful.

'She asked for you,' Elliot said, almost disbelievingly. 'At the last, it was you she wanted by your side, and not me.'

'She wanted to touch my crucifix,' Emily lied. 'She reached up for it, didn't you see her? She wanted to die blessed.'

He seemed to accept that explanation and take a little comfort from it. She told herself that a lie was not necessarily good or evil, and it did not trouble her conscience to deceive him.

It was all she could do for him now, to ease his suffering, and it seemed to her so pitifully little.

For all his profound grief, Elliot was far from a broken man. He seemed to have acquired new purpose with this tragedy, and after a minute or two of inaction, he straightened his shoulders back and took control of the situation.

'Doctor,' he said, addressing the old

man in the robe, 'you've been most kind. I realize there was little you could do to save my wife. The harm had already been done. Now I must ask another favor of you. There is a great deal that I must do before this night is over and my sister-in-law is at the point of exhaustion.'

Emily would have protested, but he silenced her with a gesture, and continued to address the Doctor. 'I think she should be taken home, but for reasons that I cannot fully explain to you, even if I had the time, I do not want her there alone.'

Whatever natural curiosity he might have experienced, Doctor Florimond was quick to put it aside.

'I will take her home for you,' he said. 'You need have no fears for her welfare.'

Elliot shook his head. 'No, I shall need the help of able-bodied men myself,' he said, 'and it would be better if you came with me to the police headquarters. In any event, you will be able to confirm some of what I will have to tell them.'

The Doctor followed his reasoning, and jumped ahead of his words. 'My wife can accompany your sister-in-law home. I assure you, she is a woman well accustomed to dealing with every sort of difficult situation.'

'It will take me no more than a moment to put on some clothes,' the Doctor's wife said, taking it for granted that the matter was settled.

Both the Doctor and his wife went off to dress. Elliot and Emily remained in the parlor. Elliot went to the sofa and, kneeling down as Emily had done a short time before, he took his wife's lifeless hand in his own. Emily looked away.

She could not bear to watch him, knowing all she knew.

Doctor Florimond and his wife were back in a very few minutes. It was decided that Elliot and the Doctor would go on into the village in the Doctor's car, and that the women would return to the house in Elliot's. Emily did not feel the need for having someone with her, but she was glad enough for the company. M. Gastion was gone, and she was sure any danger had gone as well.

At the house, she told Madame

Florimond to make herself at home. 'It may be a while before the men return,' she said.

Madame Florimond seemed quite accustomed to such nighttime activities. 'If it is going to be a while, why do I not fix us something warm to eat?' she suggested. 'I do not mind, and it will occupy us.'

Emily showed her the kitchen and left her happily rattling pots and pans. She thought to herself as she came back into the corridor that, really, a kitchen was a universal place of security. However foreign the house, the kitchen offered a sense of familiarity.

She felt restless, though, and found herself pacing to and fro. It was late, and she knew the sensible thing to do would be to try to sleep, but although she felt the strain of the past few hours, and knew she was tired, she felt not at all sleepy, and she was sure that it would be futile to retire until Elliot had come home.

Madame Lafère had apparently left the kitchen well stocked. In a short time Madame Florimond came to tell Emily

313

that she had some food ready, and it seemed to Emily she had performed wonders in the few moments she had been at work. They ate some delicately sauced asparagus on toast, and a crisp green salad, followed by some fresh berries in cream.

When they had eaten, Emily said, 'I think it only fair that I clean up.'

Madame Florimond, however, would not hear of it. 'It will give me something to do while we wait,' she insisted. 'And my husband said he thought you looked like you needed some rest. Please, leave the kitchen to me. You go make yourself comfortable.'

The trouble was, Emily thought a few minutes later, that she could not make herself comfortable. She had a feeling of incompleteness, of waiting for the other shoe to drop. She wished Elliot would return. She thought of the loss he had suffered, and her heart went out to him.

She felt her own loss keenly, but perhaps seeing the change in Irene and watching her sister during this period of possession, if that were the right term, had softened the tragedy a bit for her. She could not help but feel that Irene had already been dead to them before tonight, and that the creature who died tonight was only some demon, perhaps an extension of M. Gastion himself, although she was not clever enough about those things to truly understand it.

She could admit with all honesty, however, that she was grateful that death had occurred when it had, and that the horrible creature who had been lying on that sofa had died. And it was better for Elliot, too, that he never know what Irene had become.

Still, she could not shake the feeling that this drama was not yet ended. There was something anticlimactic in waiting like this. She was all at sixes and sevens. She could hear Madame Florimond clattering dishes in the kitchen, and she was nearly tempted to go out there and talk with her while she worked. She had the impression, though, that the Doctor's wife liked to have a kitchen to herself, and she felt that they had already imposed upon the woman's good nature as it was.

She went into Elliot's study. Near the typewriter was the stack of papers that represented Elliot's book.

She felt a pang of curiosity. Despite his total absorption in the work, Elliot had not at any time said anything about the nature of the book. She knew that he did not as a rule like to talk of whatever he was writing, and ordinarily she took this for granted, but now she found herself unaccountably curious and, hardly thinking that she was being presumptuous, she went to the desk and picked up the manuscript.

Its title was The Hiding Man. It was the phrase M. Gastion had used to refer to the darker self, the evil nature that he contended existed within every person. It was a shock to see it typed like this on the title page of Elliot's manuscript. She thought of the strange way Elliot had been possessed by this work.

She had only to read the first few paragraphs to discover that the book was about the infamous de Garacs who had lived here in this very house in the past.

For a moment she stood with the

manuscript in her hands. Someone who had come in and observed her might have thought she was listening, although the only sound to be heard was the distant rattle of dishes in the kitchen.

She went to the large, overstuffed chair and, settling herself comfortably in it, began to read.

35

Now is come a darker day,
And thou soon must be his prey.
—Percy Bysshe Shelley

It had been a nightmare for Elliot. He could not even say exactly where it had begun, where reality had blended into fiction, but the pain of the last few hours had been like the dash of cold water that brought him fully awake at last. However agonizing it might be, he knew that he was now in reality.

He could not yet fully understand all that had happened. That he had allowed this tragedy to develop without doing anything to prevent it, he was prepared to admit. Irene was dead, and he had only one purpose: that was to track down Gastion and see that he was brought to justice. Beyond that the future was a dark landscape, stretching lonely and cheerless before him, but he did not dwell upon

318

that, nor on the past. He kept his gaze fastened upon the here and now.

Florimond had rung up the station before they left his house to say that they were on their way, so that the police station was brightly lit when they arrived and there was evidence of activity inside.

A uniformed officer brought them at once into the office of the local chief of police, who rose to greet them and introduced himself to Elliot as Inspector Martell. He was a short, stocky man, with a thin sharp nose and a slightly lopsided jaw. He had the sort of exaggerated military bearing that might have been comic except for his keen eyes that gave the impression of seeing right through you.

'I'm sorry we have not met before,' M. Martell said. He waved the visitors into chairs before his desk and ordered the young officer who had escorted them in to bring them brandies. Elliot did not object. He thought a drink right now might help, and they might have a long night to get through yet.

The young man was back almost at

once with the brandies. He bent over the desk to whisper something to his chief, and after a quick nod from him, went out again, to reappear in a moment followed by the abbé.

'Father,' Elliot said, surprised to see the man of the cloth, there, in the middle of the night. 'But how . . . ?'

'Forgive me,' the abbé said breathlessly. He had a disheveled appearance, indicating he had been hurriedly summoned from his bed. 'I asked our friend, Martell, if he would get in touch with me should anything involving your house occur tonight. But tell me at once, is it your wife?'

'My wife is dead,' Elliot said grimly.

The abbé sank into a chair and took the brandy that Martell pushed over toward him. He downed it in one gulp.

'I was afraid of that,' he said.

'How did you know that something might happen?' Elliot asked. 'Were you warned?'

'Warned? Yes, in a sense. I knew . . . ah, but I did not want to face it.' For a moment, the abbé put his face in his hands as if he would weep. The room was silent but for the ticking of an old clock on a shelf. Finally, the abbé recovered.

'Forgive me,' he said. 'I will explain in due time, as much as I can explain. But first, tell me everything that has happened.'

'I don't know everything that happened,' Elliot said, 'But I'll tell as much as I can.' He began to talk in a flat, unemotional voice, as if he were reading a newspaper account. It pained him to talk of it, but at the same time he felt a sense of relief to be able to get it off his chest. His listeners did not interrupt, but sat silently, their eyes on him.

He told them briefly of having inherited the house, of traveling here to restore it, of the arrival of M. Gastion, who subsequently moved into the house as a guest.

It became still more painful as he spoke of the changes that began to occur in his wife's behavior. 'I was a fool not to realize their significance,' he said bitterly. The abbé did not interrupt but he leaned across to pat the back of Elliot's hand.

'I did not see at the time that I myself was changing as well,' Elliot went on. 'Becoming more and more absorbed in the manuscript that Gastion was helping me with. It was like he had me hypnotized, silly as that sounds. Somewhere in my mind, I knew that there was danger, that he was manipulating us for his own purposes, but still I went along with his every suggestion.'

His voice grew somewhat unsteady as his narrative went into the events of this night, but he kept his emotions in check. The listeners could see in his face what an effort this cost him.

When his story had brought him to Florimond's house, the Doctor took up the narrative and explained briefly his examination of the victim and her subsequent death.

'And now,' the Doctor said, and held out his hands palm up.

'And now,' Elliot said, 'we've got to find that monster, Gastion.' He put his hand in his pocket and brought out his gun. 'I wounded him before, but not critically, I don't think.'

Martell examined the weapon and handed it back. It was a strange story that the American had told them. He did not rule out the possibility that the man had in fact murdered his wife himself, having learned that she and their houseguest were engaged in an affair. Such things had happened before. If that were the case, however, then, where indeed was this Gastion?

'Yes, we must find him,' he said aloud. 'There are four of us here. I will have my men organize a large search party, and — '

'If you will permit me,' the abbé interrupted him. 'I think I know where we will find M. Gastion.'

The others looked at him in some surprise. Martell, who did not much like to be interrupted, remained silent.

'When we do find him, however, you will need something more than just that,' the abbé went on, indicating the weapon on the desk. He took a package and, opening it, dumped its contents atop the desk. A little pile of bullets spilled alongside the gun. Martell picked up one of the bullets, and Elliot, another.

'Why, this is silver,' Elliot said in some surprise. There was no mistaking the metal, although it had tarnished somewhat. Martell shot the abbé a puzzled glance.

The abbé nodded. 'Yes. They have been in the church for some time. They are especially blessed in the name of Saint Hubert.'

A glimmer of something broke in Elliot's consciousness. 'Wait a minute,' he said. 'Silver bullets — isn't that part of the mumbo jumbo of the Middle Ages, to kill vampires and werewolves and the like?' He looked skeptical.

The abbé remained solemn, however. 'There are more things in Heaven and earth than you or I can comprehend,' he said. 'Can you explain Gastion's presence in your house, or the power that he so obviously worked upon you and your wife?'

'No,' Elliot admitted. 'But still . . . '

'I can tell you,' the abbé went on, 'that we delude ourselves with our modern view of good and evil as philosophical abstractions to quibble with. Good and evil are realities. In the Middle Ages, men of the church knew this. It is true, there may have been a great deal of mumbo jumbo, as you put it, much myth and legend, but when we threw out all of that, we threw out a great deal of wisdom as well. The witches of the Middle Ages, for one example, possessed a very advanced knowledge of medicine and healing. In many cases, that knowledge was burned at the stake with them.'

He held up one of the silver bullets. 'These bullets are a part of ancient knowledge as well. It was believed that they were effective against such monsters as Gastion, where ordinary bullets might not be.'

'Do you think . . . ?' Elliot paused. 'Do you think Gastion is some sort of demon?'

The abbé met his gaze frankly. 'Do you think he is altogether human?' he asked.

After a moment, Elliot gave a sigh. 'No,' he said. He took one of the bullets and examined it. It was the right caliber for his weapon, and he loaded it into the revolver. The others did the same. Martell had to supply the Doctor with a weapon, and he offered one to the abbé as well, but the abbé declined.

'I have my weapon,' the abbé said. He held up a Bible. 'It is one our friend Gastion especially fears. And now, gentlemen, let us seek the demon.'

Martell said, 'I'll get some men together.'

To his surprise, the abbé shook his head. 'It will not be necessary,' he said. 'Four will be as effective as forty.'

36

*When this Mother Eve had given her
the cat Sathan, then this Elizabeth
desired first of the said cat (calling
it Sathan) that she might be rich and
have goods . . . for this cat spoke to
her, as she confessed, in a strange
hollow voice . . .*
— 'The Examination and Confession
of Certain Witches at Chelmsford in
the County of Essex before the
Queen's Majesty's Judges, the 26th
Day of July, Anno 1566.'

Queen's Attorney: 'Agnes
Waterhouse, *when did thy cat suck
of thy blood?*'
—Ibid.

It seemed to Emily as if she were reading
Elliot's manuscript with two minds. One
of them could not even quite understand
the words. They were gibberish; but the

other mind discerned sense in them, instinctively as it were. She was fascinated by the work, and sat poring over it in the flickering lamplight. She had an eerie sensation of being transported into another world, into the world of the mind. She did not so much read of these strange scenes as live them.

She became gradually aware of feeling warm, although the window was open to the night air. She stood up abruptly from the chair, breathing heavily as if she had just been running. She had changed into warm, dry clothes when she had returned to the house with the Doctor's wife. Now she found her clothing too warm for comfort.

She left the study and made her way upstairs to her room. The torn nightgown she had worn earlier was lying across a chair. She shed the clothes she was wearing and found a fresh robe among her things. It was filmy and seductive, and she was immediately more comfortable in it.

She went down again to the study, eager to return to the manuscript she had been reading. She could understand

Elliot's absorption in the work. She was fascinated by it, entranced, even.

She paused as she came into the study. The house was still. There was no sound at all from the kitchen, and she wondered if Madame Florimond had gone to sleep, but she felt no desire to go there and investigate.

She settled herself again in the large, overstuffed chair, but before she could begin reading, there was a sound from the terrace. She looked in that direction, and in a moment, a large black cat appeared. It was the one she had seen before, with Irene.

'Why, hello there,' she said, putting a hand down toward it. The cat gave a low meow and came across the room to her, jumping up into her lap. He began to purr at once, a deep, rumbling sound.

'What a lover you are,' she said, and laughed softly. How warm and sensuous the animal felt in her arms. She thought of the things she had been reading in Elliot's manuscript. Ordinarily, some of the descriptions would have shocked or even disgusted her, but instead, she had found them amusing, even arousing.

She began to read once more, but after a moment she remembered the gold crucifix about her throat. It felt oddly heavy, and restricting. She put a hand to it. It was actually irritating her throat, and the skin felt tender where the chain had rubbed it, and she wondered that she had worn it for so long without great discomfort.

'In any case, I certainly don't need to wear it now,' she said aloud. Gastion was gone, after all, and he was hardly likely to return here, to the house. Elliot had been silly to insist that Madame Florimond return with her. She was not a child, after all, who needed a babysitter.

The thought of the Doctor's wife recalled to her mind that she had heard nothing from her for some length of time. She listened intently, but there was no sound from the kitchen. She had an urge to go into that room and see if the woman was all right.

After all, though, she felt too lethargic to bother. Perhaps Madame Florimond, whose sleep had been interrupted earlier, had found someplace to take a nap. It was kindest not to disturb her.

Her attention came back to the crucifix. She remembered what importance the abbé had attached to it, but now that she looked at things objectively, she saw what an old fool the abbé was. She could not think why she herself had placed such faith in a little piece of metal on a gold chain. Of course, it was decorative. It would look very well against a black dress, she thought, but it would be insane to think it possessed some sort of protective magic. She might as well believe in voodoo dolls and witchcraft.

With a laugh at her own foolishness, she removed the chain from her throat and, on an impulse, threw the crucifix across the room, and settled back in the chair to read some more.

The black cat had regarded her somberly while she deliberated over the crucifix. Now he settled happily into the crook of her arm and began to purr again.

37

Thy corpse shall from its tomb be rent:
Then ghastly haunt thy native place,
And suck the blood of all thy race;
There from thy daughter, sister, wife,
At midnight drain the stream of life . . .
—George Gordon, Lord Byron

'Stop here,' the abbé instructed. Martell, driving the car, pulled to the side of the road as instructed.

'Why here?' Elliot asked, puzzled. They were still some distance from the house, although the road at this point went past the property.

'Because it is the closest place to where we want to go,' the abbé said, getting out of the car.

The others got out as well, and at once the abbé set off through the trees into the woods that were part of the grounds of the Château Garac. The abbé had brought a flashlight, the beam of which he kept before them, but the thin finger of light only seemed to accentuate the blackness of the night. The rain had ceased to fall, but the wind was still up.

The men were silent, each occupied with his own thoughts. The abbé's mind was filled with self-recriminations. He could see that he ought to have acted sooner than he did. He alone had guessed the truth — if it was the truth! He would know shortly, but even if he had only suspected, he ought to have done something — but what? Who would have believed him? Half of the power that the forces of evil now had was in the fact that no one believed in the powers of good.

The others had no idea where the abbé was leading them. Elliot was grim. He did not even hope to understand. What he wanted now was satisfaction. He hungered for a sight of Gastion, thirsted for an opportunity to lay his hands on the man, if man he was.

Florimond was a man of science, and it was his nature to be skeptical whenever such things as silver bullets came into a conversation. On the other hand, he had lived all his life in southern France, and it would be impossible to do that without acquiring a certain respect for the old legends.

Martell had a habit of keeping his thought processes open. He did not know yet what he believed, but he was rather waiting for more evidence. He did not put much faith in ghosts and demons. It was his experience that evil was a human invention. It was only a word, after all, that men had created to describe certain things that they did voluntarily. He had not yet discounted the possibility that the American had only wanted to murder his wife, and that the rest of it was pure fiction, but he would wait and see. If they found this Gastion, there would be some fancy questioning done, of that he was resolved.

The wind grew worse as they progressed through the woods, until it was howling and shrieking about them like a mistral. It gave the effect that they were entering the very portals of hell. Even the night seemed to grow blacker, until the flashlight beam could barely penetrate its inky depths.

Finally they broke through a tangle of growth and were in a clearing. With a shock, Elliot realized where they were. They had come to the old graveyard.

'The burial place,' he said in a cracked voice. Behind him, one of the Frenchmen whispered, '*Mon Dieu!*'

The abbé paused no more than a second at the iron railing that surrounded the graveyard. The gate at the moss-covered pillars was closed, though Elliot was certain he had left it open when he and Gastion and Irene had been here before. Someone else had been here since.

The abbé pushed the gate open. It screamed its protest, a high, wailing screech that would have sent a chill up the spine of anyone, however brave, on a night such as this.

Within the cemetery, the abbé paused again, looking about a trifle uncertainly. In the dark it was difficult to get his bearings.

'The de Garac mausoleum,' he murmured, more to himself than the others.

'Here,' Elliot said, grabbing his arm and pointing at the pseudo-Greek temple that stood by itself on the knoll. In the beam of light, they could see the moss that had overgrown the marble, and a patch of roughness where the stone had fallen away. The door still hung loose on its hinges. 'But what on earth do you think you'll find here?'

'Perhaps nothing on earth,' the abbé said. He led the way to the wide steps that went up to the iron door. 'Give me a hand with this,' he said.

The door had rusted on its hinges, so that it took their combined efforts to pull it completely open. From within came the smell of death.

For a long moment the abbé stood on the threshold of that place of decay. The wind rose up behind them, as if screaming a warning. Even Martell was chilled to the bone by the atmosphere of the place, so that he said impatiently, 'What is in there?'

'Perhaps nothing,' the abbé said. He went in, the others following close at his heels.

He flashed the light around. They saw the crypts where the de Garacs should have been laid to rest. They were empty. He shined the light on one coffin. Something scurried off to one side, but it was only a rat. The spiders and the beetles regarded them with suspicion from their places of retreat. In the faint light, the time-discolored stone, the dust and the rusty iron and tarnished brass brought home to each of them the frailty of life.

The abbé put the light on a brass plate. 'There,' he said, 'there is the coffin of the last Marquis de Garac. Go look into it, and tell me what you find.'

A short time before each of the men with him had possessed plenty of courage, but this setting — the storm outside, even the abbé's tone — robbed them of some will to act. For a long moment, none of the three moved.

Elliot at last seized his courage. He strode boldly to the coffin and looked within.

'It's empty,' he cried.

'Exactly,' was the abbé's reply. The other two men stepped alongside Elliot to see for themselves.

'Has this Gastion taken to robbing the

graves of the de Garacs?' Martell asked.

'Gastion is not his name,' the abbé said. 'He is a de Garac.'

'The descendant of the Marquis, whose body should be in this coffin?' Florimond asked.

The abbé hesitated for a moment. Then he said, 'Unless I am mistaken, Gastion is that same Marquis de Garac. That is his coffin.'

There was a chorus of gasps. Martell was shaken from his usual composure. Doctor Florimond looked as if he had been struck, and Elliot turned as white as the marble on the walls.

'Are you mad?' Martell asked. 'The Marquis has been dead for fifty years or more.'

'Buried for dead,' the abbé said, 'but not at rest, I am convinced of it. Nor do I think he died only one time. I think he might be the same Marquis supposedly buried in that coffin,' he shined his light on another, 'and that one as well. Think of his clothes. See for yourself that the tombs are empty. Come to my church tomorrow and look at a painting of the same man, a painting a half century old.'

Florimond shook his head wildly. 'No, it is impossible. Perhaps a descendant, with a strong likeness, an illegitimate child, even, who has insanely deluded himself that he is the same man — but to think that he has survived death, not once but over and over, that a man dead and buried could roam the earth, it is unthinkable.'

'And do you know everything there is to know of life and death,' the abbé demanded. 'Men declared dead by doctors have been brought back to life by medical means, and we call it an act of God. Do you not think that another power, a power of evil, might perform the same miracle? Do you think a man lives and dies, and leaves nothing behind? The history of man is filled with stories of just such creatures, allegedly come back from the dead. Do you really believe that in all those endless stories, spanning centuries and countless cultures, there is not one grain of truth?'

He went to the coffin and looked in. 'Here,' he cried, 'what's this?'

There were stains on the rotted cloth that lined the coffin. He put his finger to one of them. 'Blood!'

He turned to Elliot. 'Did you say that you wounded him earlier?'

'Yes, but . . . '

The abbé hardly waited for him to answer. He flashed the light at the floor. In its glare, they could see a double trail of stains running toward the door.

'He's come and then gone again,' the abbé said. A moment later, as the significance occurred to him, he cried, 'My God, have we come to the wrong place?'

He ran toward the door, moving with a haste they would never have imagined him capable of.

'What is it?' Elliot asked, following at his heels.

'To the house,' the abbé said. He paused at the steps and this time the light of the torch showed them what they had overlooked before — the trail of blood, going off into the woods, in the direction of the château.

'He's gone back to the house,' Elliot cried.

'Yes. Hurry, we haven't a second to lose.' The abbé rushed toward the gate and the path through the woods, and after a moment, the others followed him.

38

And he and I
Will keep a league till death.
—William Shakespeare

Emily was drifting, floating upon a dark cloud that carried her upward, high and higher, until suddenly she burst into a golden sunlight.

She blinked and opened her eyes, and the first thing that she saw was the face of Philippe Gastion. He stood over her. She had slipped down until she was lying half in, half out of the large chair. She could only vaguely remember what she was doing there. She had a half-memory of a cat, but there was no such animal to be seen now.

It occurred to her that she ought to be afraid of the man before her, but she had no sensation of fear. Indeed, she felt a certain sensuous pleasure at seeing him.

He smiled and said, 'I've come for you.' He held out a hand toward her.

She did not hesitate. Her hand came up to his and she murmured a single word: 'Beloved.'

Then she was in his arms and his lips were upon hers, and it seemed to her as if her soul fled her body.

* * *

Of all the nightmare things that had occurred and which he had still not fully grasped, nothing had filled Elliot with such horror as the sight of Emily in Gastion's embrace, kissing him. It may have been the death site from which they had just come, the abbé's ghoulish explanation as to who, or what, Gastion was. Perhaps it was the knowledge that he had lost his wife and now was in danger of losing the only other person in the world whom he loved.

Whatever the cause, and he never afterward knew it for certain, his heart stopped beating when they rushed into the room and saw Gastion and Emily together. For a moment, Elliot was frozen into immobility.

Then, with a cry like a wounded beast, he sprang into the room and seized Gastion, flinging the man away from Emily. Gastion whirled about, and for the first time Elliot saw his face.

The shock stunned him. That it was Gastion there was no question, but the man had undergone some horrible aging process. He looked just now as old as the abbé had said he was. His formerly elegant dark suit was frayed and faded, his limbs ancient and brittle, his hand a paw of parchment. Worst of all was his face, half rotted away, so that some of the bones could be seen, yellowed with age, and what skin remained was leathery and split.

The abbé cried, 'Don't let him get hold of you,' but the warning was too late. In the moment that Elliot had stood staring in horror at the creature before him, Gastion, with a snarl of rage, had leapt at him, and those bony fingers had found Elliot's throat. The gun which had been ready in Elliot's hand was knocked from his fingers and went clattering across the room.

Elliot might have expected this rotted, decaying thing from the grave to be frail, but the strength that held him now was the strength of a demon. Although he himself was strong, and he fought furiously, he saw from the very start that he was no match for his opponent. The fingers at his throat tightened, and he felt the life begin to drain from his body.

Martell had drawn his gun, and had it trained upon the two figures that danced and crashed about the room, knocking over furniture, weaving this way and that.

'Shoot him, for God's sake,' the Doctor cried.

'I cannot,' Martell replied. 'I cannot get a bead on him.'

Elliot made a desperate effort to break free. His foot slipped and he went down to his knees, his head thrown back violently so that it almost seemed his neck must snap — but the position gave Martell the chance he had been waiting for, and he took it. His gun barked.

Gastion let go of his victim and staggered backward, his hand going to his chest. He jerked about as if he might attack Martell, and nothing in that brave man's experience had prepared him for the look in the eyes that fastened on him. He had meant to fire again but he could not even hold the gun steady. Something within him urged him to drop it. He felt his fingers relax their grip.

'Shoot,' the abbé cried. He looked in Martell's direction, and at once saw the glazed stare. He threw his own arm up as if shielding himself from Gastion's gaze, and lifted the Bible in his hand, between Gastion and themselves.

Gastion snarled again in rage, but this time, he turned from them and crashed through the window nearest him. Before they could move after him, he was gone.

Martell, wakened now from the trance into which he had briefly fallen, started toward the window.

'No, wait,' the abbé said, seizing his arm. 'Let him go. We know where we will find him soon enough.'

Florimond had gone first to Emily, who was unconscious, and then to Elliot, who was getting slowly to his feet, rubbing his bruised throat. Emily gave a little groan as she began to come around.

'Help me take her into the great hall,' Elliot said to the abbé. 'There's brandy there.'

'My wife,' Florimond said, and he and Martell went in search of her. They found her unconscious on the kitchen floor, where she had fainted earlier. She too began to come around as they bent over her. The Doctor and Martell brought her into the hall also, where Elliot was just making Emily down some brandy.

'Good Lord,' Martell cried, his eyes going upward. They followed his glance to the glass painting over the fireplace.

Elliot looked too and gave a cry as if his heart had been pierced. The faces in the painting had changed. The man was unmistakably Gastion, but Gastion just as he had looked a few minutes before, rotting with age. His malevolent eyes leered down at them.

It was his victim in the painting, however, who had wrung the cry from Elliot, and who made Emily sob and cover her face with her hands.

It was the face of Irene, eyes closed,

mouth open in a final death gasp, her hair streaming behind her to catch in the thistles through which her tormentor dragged her; she was a figure to haunt one's dreams forever.

The abbé went toward the painting and reached up and put his finger to one of the crimson stains on the pale skin. He brought it away stained with blood. He turned to the horrified group behind him.

'We are not yet finished,' he said solemnly.

The others were ready enough now to follow his lead. No one argued the madness of his theories. When he ordered Martell to make a wooden stake from a piece of firewood, the policeman did so without question. Armed with this and their revolvers, the men prepared to set out again.

It was agreed that Florimond would stay with the women. 'I doubt that there is any danger here,' the abbé said. 'I think we have mortally wounded him, but we will take no chances. If anything, man or beast, comes in before we do, shoot it.'

Then he led Martell and Elliot into the

woods again, back to the cemetery. The storm had stopped, and the wind had died down. Overhead, the moon struggled to break through the clouds that masked it.

They reached the mausoleum. It took all the courage the three men possessed to cross once again over that threshold. As they did so, the moon at last broke free and sent its light over the mausoleum and into its interior. The sight that it illuminated was one that made the blood run cold.

The coffin that had been empty earlier was now occupied. Gastion — or de Garac, as they were now all willing to recognize him — had come back to his resting place. The process of aging that had disgusted and terrified them before was even more advanced. Little more than remnants of flesh clung to the bones of his skeleton. It was almost impossible to believe that this rotted corpse was the same man who had wreaked such havoc throughout the night.

Indeed, Elliot might almost have been convinced that they had made some ghastly mistake and that this corpse after all had been decaying undisturbed for decades, had it not been for what happened next.

For several minutes they stood within the threshold of the tomb. All was still. Then, slowly, as if with great pain, the head in the coffin turned toward them. The eyes fluttered open and looked with all the hatred of hell upon Elliot's face.

The abbé waited no longer. He rushed forward and with one great thrust, drove the wooden stake through the spot where the creature's heart should have been.

The night was split by a horrible shriek that echoed from the walls of the crypt. It hung suspended for a moment and was gone, and the coffin was empty save for a handful of dust.

* * *

At the house, the doctor stared in astonishment at the spot where the glass painting had hung. It had vanished in a twinkling. The wall was bare.

* * *

The three men made their way back to the château. No one spoke. The thoughts each was thinking were thoughts that no man cares to share.

As they emerged from the woods and came in sight of the château, Elliot thought of the woman waiting within. He had always cared deeply for her and been grateful for her friendship. He saw now, as if the moon had illuminated his life also, that her fondness for him had been more than that. In the wake of all this night's horror, he saw with new insight that she loved him, and always had.

He felt suddenly happy for her love. He quickened his pace.

NEW CASES FOR DOCTOR MORELLE

Ernest Dudley

Young heiress Cynthia Mason lives with her violent stepfather, Samuel Kimber, the controller of her fortune — until she marries. So when she becomes engaged to Peter Lorrimer, she fears Kimber's reaction. Peter, due to call and take her away, talks to Kimber in his study. Meanwhile, Cynthia has tiptoed downstairs and gone — she's vanished without trace. Her friend Miss Frayle, secretary to the criminologist Dr. Morelle, tries to find her — and finds herself a target for murder!

THE EVIL BELOW

Richard A. Lupoff

'Investigator seeks secretary, amanuensis, and general assistant. Applicant must exhibit courage, strength, willingness to take risks and explore the unknown . . .'
In 1905, John O'Leary had newly arrived in San Francisco. Looking for work, he had answered the advert, little understanding what was required for the post — he'd try anything once. In America he found a world of excitement and danger . . . and working for Abraham ben Zaccheus, San Francisco's most famous psychic detective, there was never a dull moment . . .